MURDER AND THE MERMAID

A POSIE PARKER MYSTERY #13

L. B. HATHAWAY

WHITEHAVEN

WHITEHAVEN MAN PRESS
London

First published in Great Britain in 2021
by Whitehaven Man Press, London

(http://www.lbhathaway.com, email: permissions@lbhathaway.com)

ISBN (e-book:) 978-1-913531-21-8
ISBN (paperback:) 978-1-913531-22-5

Also by L.B. Hathaway

The Posie Parker Mystery Series

1. *Murder Offstage*

2. *The Tomb of the Honey Bee*

3. *Murder at Maypole Manor*

4. *The Vanishing of Dr Winter*

5. *Murder of a Movie Star*

(The stand-alone novella, *A Christmas Case*)

6. *Murder in Venice*

7. *The Saltwater Murder*

8. *Murder on the White Cliffs*

9. *Marriage is Murder?*

10. *Murder in the London Lights*

11. *Murder in Tuscany*

12. *Murder in a Chelsea Garden*

13. *Murder and the Mermaid*

Friday 4th December, 1925

PART ONE

Bloomsbury, London

One

She was dreaming of the woods again, those sludgy green woods which were burned indelibly in her memory.

Winter, 1917.

Posie Parker was back in the driving seat of her trusty ambulance, and she'd reversed as far as possible near a shell-hole but the wretched vehicle had got stuck.

The slipping frozen mud of Arras had got hold of the wheels, like it had got hold of the poor desperate men, both English and German, who were flailing for their lives in it, in the aftermath of yet another battle. Men who needed help.

Her help.

But no amount of Red Cross driving lessons in the dry, cool, peacetime streets of Norwich had prepared Posie for this.

In her dream, Posie tried manoeuvring backwards, then forwards, to no avail; she felt the wheels spinning uselessly.

She tried one last time, stuck the gearstick into reverse and eased down on the accelerator – but not too much – in the cold grey light of approaching evening. Tears were not far away, and a stinging sense of failure overcame her.

Posie looked frantically in the rear-view mirror, and saw her own blue eyes looking back at her, wide and scared, no crow's feet or lines showing yet, no dark hollows shadowing the orbs of her eye sockets.

She was looking at an echo of herself, almost ten years younger than she was now, in real life.

She turned to Benny Jones, one of the volunteer Medical Orderlies, who was sitting up beside her. The two stretcher-bearers, Bill and Harry, had already got out and disappeared into the filthy grey murk, searching for the injured.

'I hate to say this, Benny, but I think you'll have to get out and push. Or we'll have to put the duckboards down. I've got us into a big old mess here.'

Benny just laughed. 'Nah, nonsense, Posie love. You can do this. You're the best driver I've ever known. Work your magic, girl.'

Benny never panicked; something to do with his former life before the Great War as a police constable on the beat in Cardiff, no doubt.

He grinned resolutely, even as the pounding of the guns began again, frighteningly close, and kept his hands fixed on the collar of his dog, Merlin, a former police dog, who, like his master, always kept calm.

'When this nightmare is all over, you'll be giving London cabbies a run for their money, an' no mistake. Now, keep your nerve and get us out of this hellhole. We've got plenty boyos to bring back in. So get us out of here, eh?'

And she had.

Sitting up with a violent, sudden start, Posie gasped aloud. Then breathed out hard to calm herself, her heart racing.

Just a dream.

Just a memory.

Even if it is one which I can't escape from.

That was years ago, another lifetime ago.

Because she was *here*, for real, lying in among the expensive oyster-coloured counterpane and rumpled sheets of her empty bed in the top-floor flat she shared with her family in Museum Chambers in Bloomsbury, hard up against the British Museum.

The room was still dark: thick curtains were drawn and a single dismal chink of grey, muted December light fell across the gorgeously-woven Turkish floor rug.

A brief glance at the luminous hands of her bedside clock told her it was already half-past seven.

The door to the bedroom was suddenly pushed open, a sliver of bright electric yellow light showing from the corridor outside, her husband's silhouette outlined there, his red hair lit up from behind.

'Darling? Everything okay? You shouted out.'

'Bad dreams again, Richard. Nothing big.'

She tried to laugh it off. 'I dreamt I was driving again…'

'Driving?'

'Mnnn. Must be those wretched sleeping powders I was given by the Doctor. I've had enough of them. That was the last; I won't take any more.'

'As you think best, my love.'

'Yes, I think it is best. You're still in your dressing gown! Aren't you going in today?'

Richard Lovelace was Chief Commissioner at New Scotland Yard, the highest rank a policeman could occupy in the land, and, in his early forties, the youngest to ever hold the position, but he hardly ever wore his regalia, preferring instead the light tweed suits in muted colours of fawn, tawny and olive he had always favoured.

'Yes, of course I'm going in. But later.'

Posie could hear the smile in her husband's voice. 'I'm having breakfast with the children. Best part of the day for me. Especially since Mrs Juniper started work here, eh? I've started on my second helpings of kippers and buttered toast already. I'm not in my suit yet as little Kit has taken to throwing porridge at all and sundry so it would be a waste of good linen. Won't you join us? Just don't wear anything fancy.'

'I'll be along in a minute.'

Resisting the urge to sink back into her pillows, Posie swung her feet onto the cold parquet floor. The thought of kippers or porridge turned her stomach, but the thought of her little family warmed her heart and spurred her on.

She could hear the babble of their voices through the still-open door.

Phyllis, her trusty and serious five-year-old stepdaughter – probably already dressed in her grey-marl school pinafore – sounded as if she was right now buttering toast soldiers for her little eighteen-month-old sister, Katie, whilst simultaneously reciting her 'ABC', trying to get the toddler to repeat it.

To say any words at all, in fact.

But to no avail.

Katie Lovelace approached life very much on her own terms, and her silver-blonde beauty and naughty-but-nice cheekiness carried her through her many tantrums which punctuated their days.

The little girl had been adopted by Richard and Posie a year and a half ago, and she was, although almost a year older than the baby of the family, Kit, undoubtedly the focal point for everyone. Somehow she had managed to make willing slaves of them all.

Kit Lovelace, red-haired and green-eyed like his father, was only eight months old but as big as a boy twice his age, and he adored his adopted sister more than anything on earth, and his gaze sought her out constantly.

Posie stood by the radiator now, pulling back the curtains, looking out at the view from the bedroom; across the jumble of angular, spiky rooftops of busy Bloomsbury, towards Oxford Street and the West End.

The ruby-red sky was vivid, ponderous, bloody; heralding a late daylight which promised nothing more than the heavy lead-coloured light which never seemed to brighten, accompanied by the ubiquitous yellow December smog.

Her thoughts were still sluggish, jumbled.

Only half aware of her surroundings, she was still thinking of her dream, and of her colleagues from the ambulance team in the Great War.

That incident she'd dreamt of, being stuck in the mud, had actually happened, and Benny Jones had indeed chivvied her on, with his talk of her becoming a London taxi-driver.

Well, that hadn't worked out, had it?

Benny was long gone, killed along with his dog, Merlin, and the whole crew, just a few weeks after Posie's own departure from the front line in France.

And as for driving, well, she hadn't sat behind a steering wheel since leaving France.

Posie leant her forehead against the condensation on the windowpane. Closed her eyes. Tried to focus on the here and now, the lovely trilling chatter of the children from the kitchen, the thought of Christmas coming.

But in her mind's eye, she could only see her hands again, on that cold steel steering wheel in France.

Hands which were younger, smoother, slimmer, with no age spots showing. Hands with no adornment, no wedding rings or engagement rings set with glittering stones.

I want to drive again, she found herself thinking suddenly, surprisingly.

I want to be free…

But why am I dreaming of France? On and on?

A past dead and buried.

Posie opened her eyes, set her shoulders squarely, scanned the beautiful room where her office clothes were already hanging for the day: a sapphire-blue thick velvet skirt-suit with a matching knitted Breton blouse tucked beneath it.

She'd bought it specially.

Today was her first day back in the office in over four months.

Posie washed quickly using the pitcher and basin and, forgetting Richard's warning about the porridge-throwing, dressed herself in her pre-chosen outfit.

She sat at her dressing table and applied powder and a dash of a brand-new scarlet lipstick, just going through the motions. Trying not to look at her big scared eyes which always looked so tired lately.

She tied on a head-sash of sapphire velvet which had black onyx-like stones sewn into it.

France.

She opened the tiny drawer beneath her oval mirror, pulled out some papers which were stuffed there; jammed in tightly, almost stuck and torn in such a confined space.

She should have thrown these away.

It was high time she did. Posie grabbed them up and marched over to where her carpet bag was hanging, and she shoved them inside.

France.

Back in the boiling, gloriously hot sizzling summer of this year, Posie had met a French boy.

And yes, he *was* a boy; no more than eighteen. He had simply been a houseguest at a place where a chilling murder had been committed, in circumstances where Posie had had to put all her professional skills as a detective to the test. Skills which had obviously impressed the boy.

He had been charming; a boy who would go far.

A boy who unabashedly liked much older women. A boy who had received no encouragement whatsoever from Posie, but had taken it into his head to write to her.

Again and again. At least twice a month.

Long letters on primrose-coloured paper with an embossed letterhead of a golden peacock had arrived at Museum Chambers. She'd intercepted and opened them all herself, fortunately. Richard had never even seen one.

But the cheek of the thing was unbelievable!

The missives had been ramblings about life in Paris,

descriptions of days spent at the Sorbonne where the boy was training to be a doctor, and careful, gentle pleadings for Posie to nip across the Channel and visit him.

The boy's name was Count Anatole de Poilac.

Posie had never once written back to Count Anatole, neither to discourage or encourage him, and she had hoped the letters would simply fizzle out, when the lad found some new object of infatuation.

She had no idea why she had kept his letters, either. She'd been flattered, she supposed. They were like a guilty secret.

Which was absolutely ridiculous! There was nothing to feel guilty about.

But she hadn't told Richard. *Should* have done, of course.

Posie vowed she'd burn the eight or nine letters when she got to work this morning. And she'd drop a single, formal line to the Count at his Sorbonne address asking him to desist from writing.

She tucked a loose wisp of a shingled brown curl under the velvet head-sash and grabbed up her carpet bag. Still she felt only half-awake; still stuck in that wretched dream of mud-covered France.

France.

Of course, there were things other than the inconsequential Anatole de Poilac which must be forcing her poor unconscious mind to revisit France in her sleep. To revisit dangerous, uncertain times.

There was, in fact, *one* other thing, to be specific. Posie sighed as she stepped out into the brightly-lit corridor, with not one child's grubby fingerprint in sight.

She stood stock-still for a moment.

Dolly.

'Oh, how I've failed you, my friend.'

Dolly Cardigeon was, or had been, Posie's best friend.

A bright, beautiful, chirpy half-French slip of a woman, Dolly had grown up in the East End of London and spoke with a broad cockney twang.

Dolly's colourful life before she had known Posie had included many things: political campaigning as a Suffragette; nursing in the Great War, and then, later, when Posie had met her, working as a Wardrobe Mistress at a West End theatre in London, which had, it turned out, been run by a bunch of criminals. But it had been a job Dolly had adored, as theatre, and the stage, and the glamour which accompanied it all, ran like oxygen through Dolly's blood.

To polish off this wonderfully disjointed string of achievements, Dolly had ended up on a high-note: spectacularly marrying Rufus, the Eleventh Earl of Cardigeon.

Dolly was now, therefore, a Countess, and the couple had three children, all under the age of five, and Dolly had access to wealth and company she had probably never thought possible.

It had been Posie who had acted as cupid, introducing Dolly to Rufus, an old Eton schoolfriend of her late brother. Posie had watched the romance – and then later, the sad unravelling of the romance – unfold.

But in July their lives had all been blown apart.

Without warning, Dolly had gone missing.

For the first couple of days, there had been mild panic and unease, but then Dolly had apparently been spotted in Paris, a city she had always wanted to visit. Dolly's long-dead mother had been a Parisian – an actress of sorts – and it was a history Dolly had always said she would explore. Dolly was also known to have a good friend, Violette, in Paris.

The trip made perfect sense. So people had calmed down. Rufus especially.

It was felt generally that Dolly might be needing a bit of a 'break'. And Rufus was, as age crept up on him, becoming ponderously dull and also very opinionated from the safety of his seat in the House of Lords, and many people had sympathised with Dolly's actions.

But Richard and Posie were far from being these people.

Richard had quickly obtained intelligence from his counterparts in Paris who claimed that Dolly had been lured to Paris by an internationally-renowned criminal gang, and that she had been captured, or kidnapped, or call it what you will, by this group. That perhaps the friend, Violette, was part of the gang.

So far, nothing had been heard directly from Dolly. The French police had had no leads, and although a daily stake-out was in place at a building on the Champs-Élysées which had been identified as being the headquarters of the gang, there were no confirmed sightings of Dolly at all.

It was all nerve-jangling, heart-stopping stuff, and Posie had vowed back in July that she would go to Paris and hunt out her friend.

She'd planned to leave almost immediately.

But then in August and September things had changed, and Posie's health had broken down. There had been an unexpected operation, a hospital stay and then a month of blustery, lonely wind-swept rehabilitation up at a hotel on the quay in Blakeney, Norfolk.

Afterwards, Posie had returned to a cold autumnal London and to her precious family.

She'd tried to focus on getting better, and lovely, worried Richard had taken her out on small jaunts, most enjoyably to the cinema to see *The Eagle*, the latest film starring Rudolph Valentino, an actor for whom Posie would always have a soft-spot.

Treats and presents had been purchased, even from America, where the make-up and fashions were really something else, but most of these remained unopened. Books had been bought, barely read; magazines discarded, left in heaps with their pages unturned.

Agatha Christie's new release, *The Secret of Chimneys,* still lay on Posie's bedside table, untouched.

This had been a time of darkness, of bleakness, of

consolidation, of seeking better, more reliable help. Mrs Juniper had been recruited as a much-needed professional Housekeeper and cook, bolstering the small household staff of Masha, the kind but erratic Russian home-help, and the Norland Nanny, who only came in for night-shifts. The running of the house, at least, was now jigging along like clockwork.

However, Posie's work at the Detective Agency, and Dolly – in Paris – had *not* been attended to. Had not been forgotten though. But had been forced by necessity to the back of Posie's mind.

Len Irving, Posie's partner at the Grape Street Bureau, was fielding all her calls and he told her he had stacked possible new cases of a non-urgent variety into a small pile on her desk at the Detective Agency.

He'd come over once a week to visit, bringing news and cheer and cakes from the Lyons Cornerhouse.

Somewhere in the flat a telephone was now ringing.

Early, surely?

It must be for Richard.

'Posie? Sweetheart?' Richard's voice sounded surprised. 'It's for you.'

'Oh? I'm coming, darling.'

She hurried along the corridor, on through the living-room, smiling and waving at the children clustered along the table in the brightly-lit kitchen which led off to one side.

Richard was standing at the open door of his study, the gold-and-black handset of the telephone apparatus in one hand, cord trailing, the receiver clutched tightly in the other hand.

'The connection's already been made by the Operator,' he whispered, frowning. 'It's the Proprietress from the Mermaid Inn, in Rye. Sussex.'

Suddenly the bleariness and heaviness which had weighed down on her since she'd woken up fled, and Posie found herself fully in the present.

Butterflies flooded her stomach and her heart started a race all of its own.

But she reached for the receiver without shaking.

'Do you know what this is all about, sweetheart?' whispered her husband.

Posie shook her head.

'No. But it's a call I think I've been expecting for a very long time.'

* * * *

Two

As it turned out, the call hadn't been the one she had been expecting for a long time. It was something entirely different. And it took under two minutes.

Posie came out of Richard's study, biting at her lip, licking off the scarlet 'Tangee' American lipstick she'd only just applied.

Her husband was perched against one of the living-room armchairs, his arms crossed, smoking fervently.

'Well?'

'It was Rufus.'

'The Earl? Oh, thank the good Lord!' Richard looked positively relieved; delighted almost, although Posie had no idea why.

'And he's all right, Posie darling?'

'Mnnn. As well as can be expected, really.'

'Has he heard from the Countess? From Dolly?'

'Directly? No. Not a sausage.'

Richard rubbed his hands through his thick hair. 'So he's down in Sussex? In Rye?'

'That's right.'

'Peculiar. Most peculiar.'

Mrs Juniper appeared, stately as a galleon in her immaculate white overall, wielding a large mug of tea which she passed to Posie, who took it gratefully and headed to the window-seat.

'Poor Rufus is tight already.'

Richard groaned. 'But it's not even eight o'clock yet. And I thought he'd put all that behind him? That those days of infernal drunkenness were a thing of the past?'

Posie shrugged in despair. 'So did we all. But staying sober was mainly attached to Dolly being with him, and now she's gone.'

Posie relayed the short conversation. Mrs Joab, the Proprietress, worried about her guest's intoxicated state when he'd appeared for breakfast, had enquired if she could do anything for the Earl.

Rufus had asked for Posie on the telephone.

And so the call had been placed, with Mrs Joab putting Rufus on the line after a short explanation.

Rufus had been hysterical: 'You will come down here, won't you, Nosy? I'll give you whatever you want: any sort of reward or payment. I need you here, *now*.'

She relayed this now to Richard, who almost choked on his smoke.

'The deuce! The Earl of Cardigeon wants you to go to Rye, in Sussex?'

'Yep.'

'But you haven't been well, my darling.'

'He says he needs me. Today. Right now if possible.'

'But *why*?'

Posie shrugged and Richard ploughed on, crossly. 'By Jove, the Houses of Parliament are still sitting! The House of Lords is in session today; he'll be missed. Good grief! He has work to do! What the blazes is Rufus doing down in Rye, at a hotel?'

Posie drank her tea in a state of high anxiety, gulping it too quickly. 'I couldn't quite work it out, Richard. But I pieced together that Rufus had been invited – or summoned by a message – to the Mermaid Inn. He was told he would receive all the answers to his questions about Dolly's disappearance when he got there.'

Richard sank down into his armchair in disbelief.

He seemed to switch off automatically from the hubbub of his children in the kitchen, ignored Masha trilling like a nervous lark above all the clamour. He stubbed out his cigarette with more force than was necessary on an old saucer and pushed it away.

He stared at Posie and she suddenly knew how it must feel to be a suspect of a horrendous crime, across the table from her husband as interrogator, ruthless as a terrier with the scent of blood in its nostrils.

'Tell me about how he was summoned to the Mermaid, Posie. *Exactly*. This all seems odd.'

Posie felt jumpy, but she didn't want to show it.

'I didn't have my notebook with me, did I? So I haven't written down the exact details, more's the pity. But I seem to recall Rufus saying something about a man called Kingsmill.'

She searched her slightly fogged thoughts. 'A Tom Kingsmill? Perhaps "Thomas" Kingsmill?'

'Kingsmill? He said "Thomas Kingsmill"?'

'Well, I think so. Rufus was gabbling I'm afraid. Drunk. Is it important?'

She watched her husband twist his lip in an effort not to bite it. His face seemed tighter, paler, more lined than it had a mere couple of minutes before. But he didn't move, didn't hurry from the chair.

And his silence and complete lack of movement worried her. After a minute or so he smiled, tightly.

'Will you go to him? To Rufus?'

'Why, yes. This *is* supposed to be my first day of work again, isn't it? So, it fits. "Work" doesn't mean I have to be in the office on Grape Street. Len can cope without me for another day or two.'

'True.'

Richard was being very supportive of this sudden and unplanned trip, Posie felt with some confusion, these thoughts overlaying her own trepidation.

She'd expected some kind of protest.

But Richard Lovelace was rising with a look of resigned determination on his handsome, ruddy face.

He turned at the door to his study. 'Good job you're already dressed, darling. Go and pack an overnight bag, won't you? I need to make a telephone call to the Yard, and dress, but I won't be more than ten minutes. We'll leave in a police car from out front. I'll get one sent around.'

Posie crossed her velvet-encased arms.

'*We?* You're coming with me?'

She felt suddenly impossibly cross, and infuriated, and worst of all, patronised. 'I can manage this alone, you know.'

Petulant now, wanting to lash out.

'He didn't ask for *you*. Rufus may have been drunk, but he knew his own mind. There was no mention of this being a police matter.'

Richard leant against the door jamb and raised an eyebrow quizzically.

'I've never doubted you can do anything alone, Posie Parker. And hell would have to freeze over before I stopped you doing anything you wanted to: that's not the man I am, and I hope you bally well know it. But you're wrong about two things here.'

'Oh? How so?' Posie jutted out her chin, her lower lip, desperate to regain some sort of moral high ground in the face of so much fairness and consideration.

'First, Rufus doesn't know his own mind when he's this drunk. And second, it *is* a police matter. I think – although I hope to goodness not – that Rufus has been lured into a trap. And he's going to need every sort of help and favour we can throw his way to get him out of it.'

Richard Lovelace disappeared for a moment inside his office, heading to the side of his room which was set out like a small library in a cosy club.

He took a moment to search the bookshelves, then grabbed at a small but thick brown-leather-bound volume.

Lovelace checked the index, then licked a finger and flicked through the pages hurriedly, catching up the telephone receiver at the same time and asking the Operator to connect him to New Scotland Yard.

Posie edged closer, rather reluctantly. Her husband shunted the open book towards her, across the tooled-leather inlay of his big partners' desk.

'See this?' he said in a low voice, his hand still covering the receiver.

'Whatever it was they taught Rufus Cardigeon at that posh school of his, it certainly wasn't history. He's been well and truly duped. Thomas Kingsmill *can't* have invited Rufus to the Mermaid Inn in Rye. Although Mr Kingsmill did know it well. Once. But Thomas Kingsmill hasn't set foot in the Mermaid Inn for two hundred years. He was a notorious, brutal smuggler. Worst of his kind. But he's dead. Hanged. Here, see?' Richard tapped at a page before giving his attention again to the call.

'What, er…sorry, Operator? Oh, yes. Of course. I want Sergeant Fox. FOX. Yes, that's right: like the animal.'

And Posie, feeling like a fool, picked up the book and turned smartly on her heel.

****

Three

It was an uninspiring book which looked like standard police fodder, entitled *Patterson's Guide to Smuggling and Tax Evasion: History and Legal Precedents.*

Dull as ditch water!

Posie hadn't bothered to read it straight away, had concentrated instead on putting some make-up and nightwear into her duffle bag, throwing on top the usual travel bits and pieces: a rope of pearls; a travel clock; a Penhaligon's bluebell-scented candle in a silver tin; a framed picture of her gorgeous children.

The brown leather book had been thrown on top too.

She'd grabbed up her new teal woollen coat which enveloped her like a cosy gauzy blanket and had skittered through to the kitchen where Mrs Juniper was wiping jam from Phyllis' face and tying her hair in neat pigtails.

Masha was clearing up what looked like a snowstorm of porridge, with Katie firmly on her hip, and Kit, ignored, had outstretched his chubby little arms to Posie, bawling loudly from his high-chair.

'Oh, lovey. Don't cry so, Kit. Mama's got to go, dearie. But I'll be back tomorrow. I promise!'

Had she imagined it or had Mrs Juniper's heavy, straggly eyebrow shot up suddenly in an arch of something like disapproval as Posie picked Kit up, covering him as she did so in a frenzy of kisses?

'Will you be all right here, Mrs Juniper? To help out with the babies, and Phyllis? I'm afraid the Chief Commissioner and myself need to leave: something's come up; a case. If you need us, we'll be at the Mermaid Inn in Rye. We *do* appreciate it. Overtime will be paid, naturally.'

A slight nod, a smile, the clipped Scottish accent deferential but knowing best: ''Course, Madam. We'll get along just fine now, so don't you worry. I'm about to take wee Phyllis to school. She'll be there nice and early, won't you, lassie?'

Mrs Juniper then nodded over to the corner of the kitchen, where a small brown dog with a red velvet bow in its hair was curled cosily in a basket with an immaculate tartan coverlet.

'But what about the wee doggie, Madam? Babies and bairns are one thing, but I'm no a real fan of doggies.'

'Oh!'

Posie blushed, ashamed. In the sudden ruckus she'd forgotten all about Patsy, her Yorkshire terrier.

'I'll take her with me. Of course!'

Posie hoped against hope that one small dog wouldn't be frowned upon or get in the way too much at the Mermaid.

And so, an hour later, Posie, with Patsy beside her on the plush seat, found herself the sole occupant of her first-class Southern Railway train carriage: the lamps burning cheerily overhead; the heater working. They were hurtling southward-bound, destined for Rye in East Sussex.

She'd spent the first minutes of the journey picking off the dried-in porridge on her coat, Kit's goodbye offering to her, and now she turned her attention to the *Patterson's Guide* which Richard had given her.

Richard himself was cloistered outside the carriage, beyond the glass doors and windows, standing in the corridor.

He was wearing a relatively smart but low-key Harris Tweed grey suit and matching felt homburg with a thick woollen black overcoat. He was speaking in hushed undertones to Sergeant Fox, who had become rather a favourite.

Fox, in contrast to his boss, looked very scruffy.

His shorn blonde hair was mussed and he was hatless, and he was sporting a rather bobbled navy duffle coat which looked suspiciously like Richard's old one from before the Great War. Fox had added what looked like a college scarf over the top – a felted creation in stinging tones of burgundy and waspish yellow – and slung on a satchel which was obviously not his own. Fox had clearly been told to dig deep in the Scotland Yard props box.

Some disguise, Posie thought to herself.

She was still uppity at having been accompanied at all on this trip, let alone by a team of detectives.

She had the nagging suspicion that Fox wasn't the only extra detective her husband had contacted today. There had been a flurry of telephone calls before they had left home, and hurried telegrams sent from Victoria Station, and Posie had a feeling he was organising something big.

Posie broke off several chunks of milk chocolate, purchased from a machine at Victoria Station. She shook her head rather crossly and attended to the book, eating at the same time.

The section Richard had indicated was very much in the 'HISTORY' part.

She frowned a little as she read:

HAWKHURST GANG AT 'THE MERMAID'

The Hawkhurst gang are probably the most famous smuggling gang in English history. Certainly the bloodiest.

Working mainly between the years 1735–1749, they

terrorised a good swathe of the south coast of England, and they were based at 'Hawkhurst' in Kent.

But for a good part of their active years, it was actually another property, this time in the thriving port town of Rye, which became their main hideout and headquarters.

This was 'The Mermaid Inn', a mysterious and legend-fuelled place located on the most important street of the town, 'Mermaid Street', a bustling thoroughfare of mainly Tudor houses which led steeply downwards to the main harbour at the bottom of the hill.

An ancient building, 'The Mermaid' was a warren of carefully-constructed hidden passageways, secret doors and trapdoors (leading to tunnels stretching out across the town of Rye) which enabled the Hawkhurst gang members to use the place freely and with a degree of brazen authority and swagger, confident they would always escape capture if Customs Commissioners ever came after them.

And while the currency of this gang were the usual commodities of smuggled tea, coffee, rum and brandy, it was the dreadful violence which accompanied their smuggling which made the Hawkhurst men so notorious.

This included bloody duels, frequent grisly murders and horrendous punishments meted out for apparent 'disobedience', such as the wholesale ransacking and setting on fire of entire villages and towns.

The leader of the Hawkhurst gang was Mr Thomas Kingsmill, and he was thankfully brought to justice and executed (by hanging) in 1749 in London.

Posie snapped the book shut.

Well, that was all very nice, wasn't it? A bit of a history lesson.

She stared out of the window, at the morning which had never really got light.

The harmonious rolling fields of Kent gave way to

flatland, then merged into the watery marshes of Sussex outside, the one county indistinguishable from the next.

Flocks of black birds, ominous somehow, sat in every bare tree which whizzed past, too cold to fly perhaps. Occasionally a village, with smoke unfurling from peg-tiled cottage roofs would be glimpsed, and in the distance, sometimes, a flock of white Christmas geese could be spied, bright against the dark green of the grass, with a lone goose-girl or boy moving about among the snowy throng.

Posie picked up her next book, a mint copy of the navy-covered *Highways & Byways in Sussex* which she'd just had time to grab at a newsstand in Victoria, while Richard was sending a telegram.

She leafed through it, and found Rye quickly, right at the back.

As Patsy snored beside her, Posie read through the guide.

A mystical, romantically-unreal town was sketched out for her, its heart beating with history. The author conjured up a vision of a citadel on a fairy-tale rocky hillock, topped by a magnificent grey church, rising up splendidly from a vast, marshy, treacherous flatland, with the sea and harbour directly off to one side.

Posie read that the town had always been a haven for smugglers who would come across the marshes at night to receive contraband cargos from the ships tethered at the busy port at the bottom of the fairy-tale hill.

But there was no mention in *Highways & Byways in Sussex* of the Mermaid Inn, or of those past, bloody smugglers.

No Thomas Kingsmill graced the pages here.

Instead, the author focused on the glories of the main church of Rye, St Mary's, with its unusual blue, cherub-decorated clock, a present from Queen Elizabeth, back in the 1500s. There was a description of the cobbled streets with their press of Tudor houses and ancient charm, and mention of the ancient Ypres Tower, which had once stood guard over the harbour.

What Posie had not appreciated was that Rye was no longer a town on the sea.

The sea was now at least a mile away, the original waterways having silted up over time, leaving Rye in all her glory trapped inconveniently inland.

Rye had lost its purpose.

Quite suddenly the door of the carriage was pulled back sharply, and a blast of cold air entered, along with Fox, who threw himself down opposite Posie. They always treated each other as if they knew each other of old.

'Wotcha, Miss!'

He got something out of his beaten-up, borrowed satchel.

'Nice coat you've got on there, Sergeant.'

'Isn't it a beauty, Miss?'

Out of the corner of her eye Posie could see Fox was rustling about with what looked like a very old book.

Posie looked quickly away and out of the window.

She could see groups of children moving in the distance, blurs in the greenish light of the watery flooded marshes. The children were heaving something along between themselves, something huge and awkward. It seemed to be an enormous freshly-felled fir tree, but it must already have been dragged a long way, for the landscape here was bleak and treeless, devoid of much life.

A Christmas tree, that symbol of hope.

Posie pressed her face against the cold window.

Christmas. That old time of wonder and renewal.

So far this year she hadn't given much thought to it at all, although Posie had noticed that the ever-efficient Mrs Juniper had put a toy catalogue from Gamages on High Holborn on top of Posie's duffle bag, presumably for perusal on her journey, and it was now stuffed, crumpled, inside the bag, as yet unread.

Posie wiped away the condensation which had formed on the glass pane, and saw the reflection of her own face looking back at her.

She got a shock.

'Oh! I say!'

'Miss?' Fox was looking over, concerned.

'Sorry, nothing at all. Don't let me disturb you, Sergeant.'

'Fine.'

The bright carriage lights behind her had thrown her face into shadows, and Posie hadn't recognised herself.

Didn't recognise herself.

Someone else was looking back at her in the glass.

Someone she had spent her whole adult life trying to forget, to blot out.

Funny really, how all these threads were coming together just now.

Posie turned abruptly from the image in the window; an image of a missing woman; a woman lost to the swirling, shifting passages of time.

Another missing woman.

But unlike Dolly, this was a woman Posie had never wanted to look for, or enquire after; even when she had been offered clues, a good lead.

A lead, funnily enough, which had specifically mentioned the Mermaid Inn, in Rye, as being a location of interest.

What a coincidence.

The lead had been given to Posie almost two years ago. But Posie hadn't wanted to pursue it.

The whole thing had been too painful to think about. Let alone address.

Rosa Parker.

Of course, this was all about Posie's mother.

A woman whom Posie had, if that reflection just now was accurate, grown to look like; the years playing a calm, cruel trick on her. It was uncanny, haunting almost.

Posie bit her lip, thoughts of her mother suddenly flooding her mind, unbidden and unasked for.

Rosa Parker, the thoroughly exotic, wholly unsuitable, half-Italian vicar's wife, who had disappeared out of Posie's life in strange circumstances on Christmas Eve, 1903. When Posie had been just eleven years old.

Rosa Parker had run away, never to return.

In all the years which followed, Rosa had never once made contact with her husband, the Reverend Parker, up in Norfolk. Nor with her son, nor with Posie.

Posie had had to navigate womanhood, and the terrors and the triumphs this brought, all by herself.

She'd never been able to forgive her mother for the desertion, but had chosen to believe, because it was easiest, that her mother was dead.

And somehow, when Posie had found out, two years back, that her mother, Rosa, might actually be alive, and had lived out a wholly-happy life with another, second family in the intervening years, it had been like a terrible slap in the face.

Posie had been glad that her brother, dead in the Great War, and her father, dead soon after from the shock of losing his only son, had not been alive to share the pain and what seemed like yet another, very fresh, stinging betrayal.

She had never spoken of Rosa Parker, of her mother – except to explain the bare bones of her disappearance – to Richard, and had never once mentioned the Mermaid in Rye as having been a place where her mother might be found.

But her evasion had been foolish: there had been a certain inevitability about the whole thing being brought out into the open as time went by, and Posie had always felt sure she would be forced to address the issue of her 'missing' mother before long.

In fact, Posie had been certain that the telephone call today, when she'd heard the caller's location, would have been to do with that unfollowed-up lead, catching up with her at last.

A point of no return.

It had been the reason her heart had thudded so loudly and painfully against her ribcage as she'd picked up the receiver; why she'd felt so awfully apprehensive as she'd started to speak. *Had she actually been expecting to speak to her mother?* To hear her voice, after twenty-two years?

Well, yes: probably.

What on earth would she have said?

It had actually been a relief when it had only been the Proprietress, wanting to put Rufus on the line.

And yet still, here Posie was, hurtling through Sussex to get to Rufus.

The result, even though it hadn't been Rosa Parker on the end of the telephone, was the same.

She was heading to the Mermaid, anyhow.

Would she find her mother now, without having actually ever planned to?

Two birds, one stone.

Posie hadn't thought through the implications of finding her mother. She'd spent so many years hating – *which wasn't good for anyone, was it?* – that the dawning realisation she might actually feel able to sit down and talk to Rosa now surprised her.

A calm, certain feeling of reconciliation seemed to sweep through Posie.

Was it actually forgiveness?

She was certain it had to do with having become a mother herself, and the understanding that goes alongside that.

The understanding that there are so many different types of mothers, no two could ever be alike.

And Posie herself was hardly the most conventional of mothers, was she? Why, she hadn't even managed to think for two seconds about what to buy her children for Christmas! And she was sure that she'd end up getting her secretary, Prudence, to organise it all in the end.

But that didn't make Posie a *bad* mother, did it? It was just her way: Posie saw that now.

Every woman had her own ways and reasons.

And so here she was; looking for Dolly, and, at the same time, looking for Rosa.

Posie realised suddenly that a lot of her career so far as a Private Detective, since she'd set up her small bureau in 1921, had been spent looking for lost men. Mainly men lost on the fields of battle during the Great War.

Now she only seemed to be looking for lost women.

Her thoughts were suddenly interrupted by a bell ringing and then the guard's clipped voice rang out clearly:

'NEXT STOP RYE! End of the line. Rye, next stop! Everyone change, please. All change.'

She turned quickly and saw Sergeant Fox watching her intently.

Fox nodded towards the window, where roads and cars and fields were still flying past but in a weird kind of slow, dragging blur.

'Cold December this one, isn't it, Miss? You were watching the snow, were you? You can't beat a bit of fresh snow. Maybe it'll be a white Christmas, eh?'

Posie turned, shocked.

She'd been so caught up in her thoughts, and that wretched blurry image of herself, that she hadn't even realised it was snowing outside. That the weird light, the smudges of scenery were due to the whirl of thick snowflakes abounding.

The snow seemed to be dancing lightly as they pulled into Rye station and harsh whistles sounded, and while the smoke from the engine cleared, outside on the platform Posie could already see her husband dismounting.

He was shaking hands in the snow with a large middle-aged man with an important-looking white walrus-like moustache, dressed in a black waterproof cape, a group of plain-clothed policemen flanked right behind him.

The man with the white moustache was handing something to Richard, looking serious.

What on earth was Richard up to? What was going on here?

Posie stood, shifting Patsy into the warmth of her carpet bag. Fox stood too, courteous, patient.

'The boss told me to help you, Miss. I'll carry your luggage, eh? Pass it over. Oh, what's this?'

Fox had spied the brown book about smuggling.

'That looks a dry old read, Miss. You should have asked and I'd have given you *my* book. It's a guide to haunted Kent and Sussex; the seller at the bookstall in London swore by it. Maybe he thought that's what down-at-heel students like me enjoy reading, eh?'

Fox shunted Posie's duffle bag easily.

'We're in for a treat, Miss. Turns out this 'Mermaid' place we're going to is one of the most haunted spots in the British Isles. Exciting, isn't it? At Christmas, too! There's always something very satisfying about a ghost story at Christmas, don't you think, Miss?'

'Fan of M. R. James, are you, Sergeant?'

Fox laughed and nodded, and they headed down the corridor.

'The Mermaid is more than a story though, Miss. It's downright creepy. There's a glass bauble in every single room in that place, with the intention of reflecting ghosts' reflections back at themselves and thus scaring them off. So, in addition to hunting for the Countess of Cardigeon, and looking out for the Earl's well-being, we'll have some proper spooky company at our lodgings.'

Fox made a slight 'woo-hoo!' noise and mock-shivered.

'So we can't get too comfy, eh, Miss? In fact, the book at Victoria Station was a bit of luck: the boss told me to come undercover – *any* cover – and I came as a student but I think I'll pretend to be a ghost-hunter instead. It seems more convincing. The place is apparently chock-full of ghosts.'

Posie snorted in disbelief.

'Where *isn't* these days?' she retorted tartly.

Ghosts, not that she believed in them, had never bothered her.

No: it was the living who could, and *did*, inflict real pain, which sometimes, and inconveniently, threw long shadows back through the past and on into the future.

****

PART TWO
The Mermaid Inn
(Rye, Sussex)

Four

The snow was falling heavily from a clay-coloured sky as Posie and Richard walked the ten-minute route to their destination. Posie carried Patsy in her folded-up carpet bag, buried deep in the folds of her big coat, to keep the small dog warm.

Behind them loped Sergeant Fox with his scruffy satchel and the luggage, and beyond him again, the gaggle of men from the station, whom Posie could only presume were plain-clothed policemen, working on Richard's instructions.

As they walked, the bitingly cold air and uphill cobbled streets put a flush in Posie's face and a resolve in her heart.

She felt more alive than she'd done in months, and it felt amazingly good.

Second by second, she felt as if she were coming back to herself.

Going uphill, Posie saw the medieval walls of the town in a kind of blur, noting the well-dressed shoppers on the smart, glossy High Street which they suddenly came out upon; the fashionable glass-fronted cafés and art galleries and select boutiques which were fit to bursting with ladies taking cover from the snow.

Posie paused for a moment outside a small art gallery, sheltered in its overhang.

The entire front window was taken up with a framed painting of the town on a hot summer's day.

Ant-sized people thronged the streets of Rye in the painting, which was portrayed in dollhouse-sized miniature, and tiny silver mermaids were frolicking in the shimmery sea which circled the entire picture. A tiny fashionable crowd stood on the quayside, and a couple, the woman in purple, the man in brown, were dancing on the cobbles. The painting made Posie feel calm somehow, and she smiled before moving on.

A group of workmen were starting to string up white necklace-like Christmas lights across the street, and shiny black motor-cars were parked all along Rye High Street, their beetle-like bodies snow-flecked.

What was it which drew my mother here, if indeed she is here? Posie wondered to herself, hardly noticing the chill.

Muddling the route somehow, they ended up passing the white, prestigious pearl-like Georgian façade of what looked like a classy sort of hotel, and Posie saw a shiny bronze plaque announcing itself as '*The George Hotel – Assembly Rooms and Musician's Gallery – Dancing Daily.*'

Through the glass mullioned windows Posie saw women of around her own age in candy-coloured flimsy *crepe-de-chine* dresses standing about languidly: smoking, laughing, holding coffee cups daintily. An unreal reality.

'Quite some place this, eh?' muttered Richard in rather approving tones, squinting through the snow, which fell and landed in his long eyelashes despite his homburg hat.

They trudged up Lion Street, all steeply uphill, formed of slippery cobbles, passing bookshops, and restaurants filling up for early lunches.

They were headed for the peculiarly dominant church at the top of the hill, which seemed to look out all over Rye, like some sort of glowering beacon.

'We've gone the wrong way, the deuce!' said Richard, coming to a sudden stop outside the church. A carefully-painted board read: 'ST MARY'S CHURCH, RYE.'

Richard looked back at the supposedly-inconspicuous policemen and the one with the big white moustache pointed a stabbing finger to the right, indicating they should go on through the snowy churchyard.

Posie glanced up at the blue clock on the church supported by its two fat golden angels, and its hands which indicated it was a quarter-to-twelve, and she saw a crowd of young boys, motley-looking, wet and shivering, gathered around a still-bare Christmas tree, as yet undecorated, which was being put up in the churchyard, outside the church door.

She wondered if the boys, too young to have known the horrors of the Great War, had ever glanced upwards, still less appreciated the golden biblical inscription on the clock above them.

'FOR OUR TIME IS A VERY SHADOW THAT PASSETH AWAY.'

'Darling?'

Posie must have been staring, for Richard looped his arm through hers and they started off again, passing the now-white higgledy-piggledy mass of old lopsided graves, stepping out onto a cobbled path which hugged a line of old Tudor buildings, leading into tight lanes of yet more bookshops and pawnbrokers.

'Are you feeling just the ticket, Posie?'

'Never better, love.'

'Good, good.' But Richard didn't sound convinced.

'But what exactly are you doing with all these fellas, Richard? Rufus is only expecting *me*. I didn't even tell him you were coming. I thought you were only bringing Fox. This is overegging the pudding somewhat, isn't it?'

Richard's face looked grim and he flicked the snow away in a determined manner.

'This could be big, Posie. Very big. It's the only "lead" we've had on the whole missing Countess of Cardigeon story in weeks. Months, really.'

'But, darling! It's just Rufus, probably having a boozy breakdown of some kind! He needs a friend who cares, not an entire battalion of police!'

Richard shook his head, steering Posie along the snowy street where an icy wind was blowing.

'No, Posie. Here you are wrong. There's this letter, this message, isn't there? This invitation to Rufus? A fake enticement from a suspicious person called Thomas Kingsmill, who's been dead for two hundred years. It's mad! Not to mention fishy as hell, believe me. And why *here*? Why is Rufus here? In some godforsaken backwater, lost to the mists of time? A place which is cut off; in the marshes; a haven throughout time and history for smuggling and smugglers. A place with direct access to the sea. A gateway to *France*! In fact, did you know that as the crow flies, Rye is actually closer to France than it is to London? It's perfect if you want to get someone away in a hurry.'

Posie scowled.

She hadn't actually for one moment put any of this quite sensible deduction together; hadn't thought the whole situation through. And she hated being late in on anything.

'So you think the same gang who may be responsible for Dolly's disappearance – *if* that is what has happened – are here in Rye trying to involve Rufus in some capacity? But how? Why?'

Lovelace stopped, threw a look over his shoulder, nodded and then marched on. He lit a cigarette as he walked.

'Ah, here we are! Mermaid Street, thank the Good Lord.'

'You were saying, love. About *Rufus*...?'

'Sorry, Posie? What? Er, yes, Rufus. Well, I'm not sure of anything of course. But Rufus Cardigeon is one of the richest men in the country, isn't he? Richer than

Croesus by all accounts. So, I'm willing to bet my Chief Commissioner's badge that he's been enticed here in a trap. That the gang who are holding Dolly Cardigeon will use her as some kind of bait in order to secure a massive amount of money from her husband before returning her. *That's* the best-case scenario.'

Richard took a deep drag of his cigarette, blew out wearily.

'Another scenario is that they secure the money but *don't* return Dolly. And the very worst scenario is that they will simply lure Rufus off somewhere, perhaps on a small boat across these dratted marshes, with the promise of meeting Dolly at the end of it. In France, perhaps. And then that scenario ends with both of the Cardigeons going missing; two high-profile personages lost and us being none the wiser as to what the blazes is going on here.'

They had stopped in the middle of the cobbled street, which was just as well as Posie's heeled, blue-velvet Mary-Janes probably wouldn't have managed much more of the slippy, treacherous unevenness. They felt a little damp.

Behind them loomed the Mermaid Inn, and first impressions were impressive.

It had a white-and-black beamed exterior and a prominent metal sign showing a golden, curled mermaid trapped within the confines of a black cage.

The entire exterior was snow-dusted, with lights burning brightly behind the many gleaming diamond-paned windows, some inlaid with stained glass, which flashed like blazing gems.

Deep in Posie's thick coat Patsy sniffled and moaned. She hated the cold, and even watching snow fall seemed to make her uneasy.

Posie stared up at her husband now, right into his beautiful, speckled green eyes, which were quite his best feature, and he held her gaze, smoking all the while.

She spoke at last, quietly, calmly. 'I agree with your

hypothesis. But I'm going to turn the tables on you here: you're always on at me about "evidence". Surely your feeling about what's happening to Rufus is founded on more than a hunch? Do you have any evidence?'

Richard Lovelace nodded grimly. 'Yes, there is evidence.'

He brushed the snow away from his coat lapel and pulled out two telegrams.

'I know better than to go in all guns blazing on nothing more than the mutterings of a drunken man, even if he *is* an Earl. Before we left on the train I called through to the Sussex Police Force and I asked them to see if anything odd was going on here, and to intercept any messages which might be leaving the Mermaid. Inspector Vallance of the Rye branch managed to get copies of *these* telegrams which were cabled out from the main town Post Office early this morning. They were placed and paid for by a Monsieur Francois Redon, a guest staying here at the Mermaid. Vallance gave me these at the train station, just now.'

Posie read the telegrams quickly.

The first read:
ILS DISENT QU'ILS ONT COMPRIS
And scrawled beneath was someone's pencilled translation:
'THEY SAY THEY HAVE UNDERSTOOD.'

And the second read:
QU'IL N'Y A PLUS LE CHOIX
And the translation:
'THAT THERE IS NO MORE CHOICE.'

Posie looked incredulous, shoving them back at her husband.

'But these mean nothing! Less than nothing, Richard dear. They could be about anything at all. The price of fish, even!'

'Cryptic, though, aren't they? They *could* mean a good deal.'

Posie scoffed, walking to the red-brick steps to the inn, directly below the sign of the curled-up mermaid.

'And does this Monsieur Redon have any known connection to Rufus, or are you just picking on him because he's French, and it fits what we think we know already about the Paris gang?'

Richard crowded onto the step next to Posie. He hissed in her ear: 'Look, I didn't tell you this earlier, darling, because I thought it might worry you. But late yesterday afternoon Rufus Cardigeon's newest navy Lagonda was found crashed off the cliffs at Hastings, and there were suitcases and all sorts strewn about the place. The car itself was already half-submerged in the sea, with the tide coming in when the call came in. There wasn't a hope of getting at it last night. The light was already failing. Must have happened at about three-thirty.'

'*What?*' squeaked Posie in disbelief.

She took a deep breath. 'So *that* was why you sounded so relieved when I said it was Rufus this morning on the telephone; you thought he'd killed himself by driving off a cliff! Good grief! And you didn't tell me?'

'You haven't been well, sweetheart, and I had no body, no nothing. No proof, no evidence. I've had the devil of a time keeping it out of the papers. Hushed it all up. But it's all jolly odd. Hastings is not far from here, is it? Perhaps only twelve miles along the coast?'

He cleared his throat uneasily, in readiness to go in, then indicated Posie should push open the black wooden front door, which she refused to do, despite shivering violently now.

'What else is there, Richard? I know you very well, darling, and there's something else you're not telling me. Come on: spit it out.'

Richard shrugged resignedly. 'Sussex Police have reports of a woman standing on the cliff at Hastings, dressed oddly, watching the car wreck out at sea for several hours yesterday, even after dark. I'm wondering if it could be this French girl, Violette? The woman involved in Dolly's disappearance? The woman looked exotic apparently, foreign.'

Foreign.

Such a description seemed ludicrous.

And Posie rolled her eyes.

* * * *

Five

Inside, the hotel was cosy, low-beamed, with red carpets throughout and ancient inscriptions lingering on the walls. It was probably the oldest place Posie had ever visited.

'Miss Parker?'

The Proprietress, Mrs Joab, a smart blonde in a burgundy city dress, had obviously been awaiting their arrival, and she looked happy to see Posie. She had clearly been forewarned about Richard's arrival with the police, too.

'The Earl is asleep, upstairs, Miss Parker.'

The woman passed across a room key. 'Perhaps you'd like to go up to your own room until he's up again? I've put you both in…'

'We need to wake the Earl up, Madam,' cut in Richard urgently, 'and quickly.'

'Of course, sir. I'll go up immediately.'

Richard was now asking if a Mr Redon was staying at the hotel, or if there were any other French guests, come to that.

'Mr Redon? Why, yes, of course.'

'Is he here now?'

The Proprietress looked confused, but checked her watch. 'No, Chief Commissioner. He seems to like eating fish and chips down by the quayside: it's his treat. Quaint, really, isn't it? If he does the same as yesterday, he'll be back here in the early afternoon.'

'He eats outside? In the cold? In this snow?'

'Apparently.'

'I see.' Richard seemed relieved. 'And the Earl? His room is secure, is it?'

'Secure, Chief Commissioner? How do you mean?'

'I mean, are there any hidden passageways connected to his room? Or tunnels? Or Priest's Holes? I hear the Mermaid is famous for them.'

And then Posie watched Richard get into a blind panic on hearing that Rufus was staying in Dr Syn's bedchamber, a big grand room directly above them, facing out onto Mermaid Street; a room complete with a hidden bookcase which led to a secret staircase spiralling down towards the main bar of the hotel.

Richard was charging off outside, into the snow again, giving instructions to the plain-clothed Sussex policemen; telling them to secure all of the exits and entrances to the hotel.

The man with the big white moustache was looking important, taking up his own position across the street.

Posie went through to the small, empty, wood-panelled lounge opposite the reception, where a welcome fire was burning in the grate, and she saw that another receptionist, a middle-aged man with dark hair, had taken over at the front desk, and was checking Fox, the so-called 'ghost-hunter', in; taking his money and identity papers and handing over a key.

She'd just settled into an easy chair near the fire, relieved to finally be warm, and she'd shaken Patsy out onto the floor and was leafing through an illustrated catalogue about the hotel, when the male receptionist came through. He was bearing a tray with a pot of hot coffee and a plate of shortbread biscuits.

He introduced himself as Evans.

'A hot luncheon will be served soon in our restaurant, Madam,' he said politely. 'And Mrs Joab has gone to tell the Earl that you have arrived. He'll be down in a minute.'

'Thank you. I'm wondering, Mr Evans, why is the hotel here called 'The Mermaid'?'

Posie motioned towards the catalogue. 'Is there a particular reason? I can't see anything about it here.'

Evans beamed, happy to chat. 'We don't know why exactly, Madam. But as this was a port, and a sea-faring town, folks think the hotel here was named for a ships' prow, carved like a Mermaid, brought up from one of the boats, for good luck. Most likely it was affixed to the roof of the Inn in the days before the Tudor Kings, but the place was burned to the ground at least once, and the lucky Mermaid disappeared.'

Evans shrugged. 'Still, I reckon when the legend of something is strong enough, it doesn't matter if the original is long gone. It lives on anyhow.'

'Mnnn. Very true.'

Evans coughed delicately, as if broaching a difficult subject. 'I hope you don't mind my asking, Madam, but have you ever stayed with us before?'

Posie tried her best, winning smile. 'No, this is a first for me. I'm very excited to be here.'

Evans looked puzzled for a second or two. 'Oh! Oh, how odd. Forgive me; I thought I'd seen you before. Or else, you remind me very much of someone, but for the moment I can't think who. Well, if you need anything, you know where to find me.'

Posie wolfed down the shortbread, licking her fingers greedily like a cat.

The bites of chocolate on the train seemed a long time ago now.

My mother has or had a connection with this place, Posie reflected.

I was told that two years ago.

And this fella, Evans, must be reminded of my mother, Rosa, when looking at me. Like I reminded myself of her when I saw my reflection.

So the 'lead' two years back must have been good; Rosa Parker must be, or *have* been here. And this knowledge sent a slight shiver of excitement up and down Posie's spine.

Posie felt certain of the way forward now. *I'm going to sort out Rufus, then nip this whole 'missing mother' affair in the bud.*

But then came a wrenching, slamming noise overhead, of wood hitting wood, and the unmistakeable BANG BANG BANG of Rufus Cardigeon's steps on an ancient staircase, descending. Loud despite the carpeting.

Rufus, Eleventh Earl of Cardigeon charged through into the small lounge, a blur of lolloping tweed and straining buttons and pure despair.

'Oh, Nosy! Thank heavens you came!'

He crashed into Posie, enfolding her in a bear hug and waves of a whisky fug enveloped her.

Discreetly, over his enormous shoulder. Posie saw the door being closed behind them by the Proprietress.

Rufus Cardigeon had been a slip of a lad, a tiny boy, back in the days when he had been the best friend of Posie's brother at school. Now, as he nudged his forties, he was massive, becoming a carbon copy of his late father, whose bulk had been legendary. Rufus was sweaty and almost bald on top and today he had a haggard, ashy expression.

He released Posie at last, and sank down into the other armchair. His big meaty hands were trembling violently.

'What's going on, Rufey?'

'I could ask you the same thing, old gal. By Gad, it's been ages since we met last: it was around the time Dolly vanished, wasn't it? Summer? Must have been, there were all those pictures in the newspaper of you and I together, outside my house, caught in the flash-light, looking worried, wondering how best to get Dolly back. They all said I'd consulted you professionally! Pah!'

Rufus shook his head wearily. 'But you look terrible, Nosy, you're all bones; I barely recognise you. What happened?'

Posie's stomach lurched. She hadn't been ready for these kinds of questions yet. Fortunately, Rufus was ploughing on, agitated:

'Besides, I asked *you* to come here today to me, not send in the bally troops. Caught sight of old Richard outside just now, what? Like he was going off his head with worry, eh? And he's got a load of rozzers here too by the looks of things! But *why*?'

Posie succinctly explained Richard's fears. They sounded pretty convincing when spoken aloud, actually.

And then she mentioned the crashed navy Lagonda, and its watery resting place, and watched Rufus stagger up from his chair in open-mouthed horror, and rub his hands over his eyes, then dig in the inside pocket of his tweed blazer for a silver hip-flask.

He took a deep swig, wiping his mouth clumsily, heading for the bay window with its three diamond-patterned panes.

'By Gad, a fix? A *trap*?'

He stared out over the cobbled street, and Posie rose to join him. 'But, oh! First Dolly, and now my lovely Lagonda…'

Posie was about to snap that surely there was no comparison between losing a wife and losing a car, but she bit her tongue and made sympathetic noises. 'I know, I know. I always rather fancied driving a Lagonda myself… but tell me exactly why you are here, Rufus. Do you have a connection to the Mermaid, or Rye?'

Rufus shook his head, panting with the effort of simply standing still.

He turned blearily to Posie. 'Never been here before in

my life, old chum. Lovely place and all, but if I want old ship's beams and large Tudor fireplaces with a few ghosts thrown in for good measure, I just motor on up to Rebburn Abbey, to Yorkshire. You know?'

Posie nodded. Oh, yes: she knew. The Cardigeon ancestral pile. She'd had her fair share of cold nights up there.

Rufus waved his hip-flask. 'I certainly wasn't planning a trip away. But yesterday, just after one o'clock, at the House, I was asked to come out of the chamber during a fixed debate, urgently, and my secretary handed me a telegram, basically telling me to get down here to this jolly old joint. It was from a fella called Thomas Kingsmill. He told me there would be answers to be had about Dolly's disappearance. Even mentioned the exact Southern Railway train to get on at Victoria; the one forty-five!'

Rufus took a few gulps of the drink, wiped his mouth quickly.

'Well, you can imagine, I darn well hurried along like a bird on the sprightliest of wings. Didn't go back into the chamber even for a second; told my secretary to book me the best room here at the Mermaid, and then I telephoned home for my Butler, Partridge, to hot-foot it to Victoria with a case of my clothes, and a change of clothes for Dolly, just in case she appeared down here. Like magic…'

'I see.'

Posie was studying the white house opposite, which seemed to gleam through the snow at her.

Was she going mad? There were two identical black glossy doors, both adorned with golden dolphin door-knockers. A sign declaring 'THE HOUSE WITH TWO FRONT DOORS' was painted there.

Everything in this town was slightly odd.

The policeman with the white moustache was still there on the double-width doorstep. Sentry-like, gathering snow.

'Is the Butler your only staff at present, Rufus?'

'Yep, apart from the Housekeeper, and she's just a daily help. Only comes in for the morning. Doesn't seem much point keeping a full staff on with Dolly missing and the children up in Yorkshire at Rebburn with the Nanny and Governess.'

'Quite.'

Rufus took another swig of the whisky, and then he brought out one of his usual cigars. 'But why this sudden interest in my domestic arrangements, Posie? How does that help us?'

Posie shrugged. 'It doesn't. But it means that whoever took your Lagonda from your garage at your house on Pavilion Row in Chelsea was able to do so very easily. *You* were out, and then so was Partridge, when he went to Victoria with your valise. He was gone for a good hour I expect, doing that. And probably the lock on your garage is easy to pick. Although it does seem jolly odd that your Butler hasn't called here yet to tell you about the missing car...'

Rufus lit the huge cigar, inhaled deeply. 'Not really. Between you and me, Posie, Frank Partridge is not first-class Butler material. He was a gunner in one of my old battalions in the Great War, and I felt sorry for the lad, so I gave him employment. He was injured pretty badly, as it happens.'

Rufus tapped the silver flask beside him meaningfully. 'I think Patridge hits the bottle as hard as I do, to be honest. To forget, you know...' He trailed off miserably. 'I told him I'd be gone for one night, and I expect he used the chance to have the evening off; have a few sherbets.'

Rufus glanced at his handsome Rolex wristwatch. 'I expect Frank will only just be waking up about now, so he won't notice anything is amiss for a good while yet.'

Posie nodded. Out of the corner of her eye, she'd caught sight of a large green glass bauble, much like some sort of expensive Christmas tree decoration, hanging in the corner of the room, near the fireplace. This must be the kind Fox had been telling her about: superstitious trinkets to ward off ghosts. This one showed her and Rufus clearly in it, but their figures were distorted and eerie.

But there seemed to be someone else reflected in the bauble.

Was she imagining it, or was there a woman – dark, elegant, slightly sparkling – standing over by the panelling, near the door? There was a flash of silver somewhere, glinting; a bright stab of light, as if caught between the wooden panelling.

Posie whirled around but there was no-one there. The silver had been a trick of the bad light.

Reflections.

Buck up, she told herself robustly.

'And you got here yesterday with no problems, Rufey? Had dinner here at the Mermaid? Slept well? No-one has bothered you? Met with you?'

'I got here just fine, old girl. On arrival I asked if there was a lad called Thomas Kingsmill waiting here to see me, and I must say I got a dashed funny look from that nice Proprietress, but he hasn't shown up yet, if he's coming at all. And dinner was first-rate. I slept like a log, too. Probably because I tried almost all of the malt whiskies in the Giant's Fireplace Bar before bed, and they were all jolly good, as it happens.'

'You sound like you're having a mini holiday here, Rufus,' Posie said, slightly spitefully. 'So, if the stay was so relaxing, why the panic and rush to call me this morning? Get *me* down here?'

Rufus looked sheepish, tapped some ash from his cigar into a small green glass ashtray with a gold stencilled mermaid upon it.

'Ah, well, I messed up, actually, Posie. There had been a second telegram from this Kingsmill chappie, actually. It was on my desk upstairs here all the time; must have been there already when I arrived yesterday. But I somehow overlooked it; must have thrown something down on top of it. I only saw it this morning. It was the second telegram which made me call for you.'

'What did it say?'

'Oh, hang this for a laugh, I'll go and get them both, shall I?'

'Might be easiest.'

Alone, suddenly, listening to Rufus' clumping footsteps going upstairs again, Posie watched without properly seeing as men with greenery and Christmas decorations thronged through Mermaid Street outside.

'Do you mind if I interrupt you, Miss Parker?'

It was the Proprietress at the door, Mrs Joab. 'Your table is ready in the Linen Fold Restaurant next door, Miss Parker, and your husband says he will be joining you in a minute.'

The woman was holding a newspaper in her hands, the *Sussex Express*. 'I wondered when you first came in, and now I feel sure, that you must be Rosa Rossoli's daughter. The resemblance is very striking.'

'I…' Posie's breath trailed away. She felt as if her stomach was suddenly full of ice, but she forced herself to sound professional.

'I'm afraid I haven't spoken to my mother in many, many years. Not really out of choice, though. You know her, do you, Mrs Joab?'

'*Know* her? Ah, well, Miss Parker, I wasn't sure if you knew. Obviously not…But your timing is really uncanny…'

The newspaper was shaken out, pages swiftly turned. Mrs Joab smiled in a reassuring but worried sort of way.

'I *did* know Rosa, yes. I employed her, as it happens. For many years. More than twenty, I suppose. I employed both her and her husband, Benito. They worked here: both of them were well-loved dancers and they organised popular tea-dances in the summer season, and then they helped out with pretty much everything else all through the wintertime. They had a little daughter, Dulcie; she grew up here. They lived here, too, upstairs, in a small staff apartment. It was a perk of the job.'

Mrs Joab sighed. 'And that was the case until Benito died a couple of years ago. Rosa didn't want to carry on here alone; she'd lost all heart. So she handed in her notice last year, decided instead to teach afternoon slots of dancing at The George, down the road. But she kept her apartment upstairs, I insisted. Sometimes Rosa came down here, into the main hotel itself if we needed an extra hand in the restaurant, or help in the kitchens. And once a week, regular as clockwork, she used the telephone in reception for making one call.'

Mrs Joab handed the newspaper across.

'Here. I hope you find what you're looking for, Miss Parker. This is Wednesday's edition.'

And then suddenly she was gone, and Richard was back, his face red and raw with cold, warming his hands by the fire, and Rufus was calling.

Posie found herself being herded along red-carpeted corridors, past dried swathes of hops and random busts of Shakespeare, and past wrought-iron partitions.

They came out into a long, low, oak-panelled room with another magnificent blazing fire. This room was obviously the restaurant, packed with tables, the white tablecloths immaculate as the snow outside.

At the other end of the room, beneath a shiny red ghost-repelling glass bauble, Sergeant Fox was concerned with more down-to-earth matters, and was already attacking a generous plate of eggs Benedict, with several rounds of toast.

And Rufus was calling for a bottle of Krug 1920, and waving telegrams in his hand.

Telegrams as mysterious as the newspaper which was now stuffed, alongside Patsy, in Posie's old carpet bag.

And Posie felt a sense of trepidation growing, minute

by minute, in this strange, lovely place which seemed chock-full of secrets.

* * * *

Six

As Rufus poured the champagne and the clock struck half-past twelve, Richard and Posie read the telegrams which had been sent to the Earl. They were short.

Both had been sent from Rye Post Office. At just before one o'clock the previous day, Thursday.

The first, sent to the House of Lords yesterday, read:

YOUR GRACE,

ANSWERS ARE TO BE FOUND AT THE MERMAID INN, RYE, SUSSEX ABOUT THE DISAPPEARANCE OF YOUR WIFE.

THE 1.45 FROM VICTORIA TODAY IS THE LAST TRAIN TO ARRIVE IN ABSOLUTE DAYLIGHT.

I LOOK FORWARD TO MEETING YOU,

THOMAS KINGSMILL

And the second, sent at exactly the same time, but to the Mermaid Inn itself, read:

YOUR GRACE,

IT WOULD BE BEST IF POSIE PARKER, THE PRIVATE DETECTIVE, COMES HERE TOO, TO FIND OUT WHAT HAS HAPPENED TO YOUR WIFE.

I WILL LOOK OUT FOR YOU BOTH AND INDICATE MY PRESENCE AT THE EARLIEST OPPORTUNITY,

THOMAS KINGSMILL

Richard scowled and looked over at Fox and whistled. Fortunately, so far they were the only diners in the restaurant.

Fox sauntered over languidly, satchel in tow, and Richard hissed at him to abandon his meal and get down to Rye Post Office and find out which Telegraphist had cabled the two messages to Rufus yesterday at one o'clock, and, once found, to interview the Telegraphist about the identity of the actual sender.

'And if you then find the person who sent the telegrams then throw the bally law book at them, Sergeant. Threaten everything you can. Arrest them if you have to.'

'Sir? Would it be more helpful if I bring them back here? Low-key, like?'

'Perhaps.'

Richard handed the telegrams to Fox as if they were toxic, and almost growled: 'Just act quickly, lad. And find out what's happened to His Grace's car at Hastings; if it's been dragged up out of the sea yet, eh? The tide will have turned by now...'

Once they'd ordered their meals, and refused Rufus' offer of champagne, Richard started to crack at his knuckles, which was always a bad sign.

'What's wrong, darling?' hissed Posie, almost under her breath. 'What's changed since we got here? You're even more on edge than you were before.'

'*Something*. But I'm not sure what. I feel as if I can't see the woods for the trees. It seems as if the game has changed. But I don't know *how*.'

And then the usual questions ensued for Rufus to answer: had any man approached him since his arrival here? Could there be any further messages he might have 'overlooked'? Had he been in contact with anyone – man or woman – of French nationality in the last couple of days?

To all of these Rufus replied in the negative.

Two steps forward; *three steps back*, thought Posie to herself wearily.

As her Rye Bay scallops with fried onions and mashed potato arrived, and she felt a hunger she hadn't in a good long while, Posie threw out an idea which had been suggesting itself as a possibility to her ever since she'd stepped inside the hotel.

'Is it surely not just possible that this is some sort of horrible person's good idea of a practical joke? Someone with a grudge to bear, Rufus? A disgruntled employee, or another Member of the Lords, or Parliament, whom you've fallen out with? Some recipient of your largesse which may have dried up for one reason or another? Some dreadful person who thinks it's really all right to capitalise on the suffering of another person?'

Rufus snorted. Started to cut up his steak – rare, local – meticulously.

'Hardly! I haven't fallen out with anyone lately, Nosy. Actually, nearly everyone – even former enemies – has been most kind.'

'So, tell me, Rufey, do you *really* think this Thomas Kingsmill chappie is going to show up?' Posie ventured, eating mashed potato. 'As and when he wants?'

Rufus shrugged. 'Hopefully. Otherwise we're all wasting our time, aren't we?'

Richard groaned, pushed his delicious meal away, virtually untouched. 'Something here is not right, not right at all. But what is it?'

You mean you hope it's something, thought Posie, rather uncharitably, eating on.

With half the town's police force here, stationed about the place in an Arctic chill, twiddling their thumbs, waiting for action, it won't look good if this was all for nothing...

Richard ran his fingers through his thick mane of red hair. 'Your Lordship, have you ever even heard of Thomas Kingsmill before?'

Rufus looked up, stumped. 'No. But I thought that would be your job, Richard old buddy. Isn't that why you've come here? That you'll find this chappie and force the information out of him, one way or the other, eh?'

'We're two hundred years too late for that,' muttered Richard, disconsolately. And it was as if all the fight had gone out of him.

****

Posie was up in her cosy, wood-panelled bedroom, where she told Richard she'd gone to rest, but really, she was up there to read the newspaper she'd been given before lunch by Mrs Joab, which she hadn't been able to stop thinking about all through luncheon.

Richard told her that he'd remain downstairs, in the Giant's Fireside Bar.

This was an ancient, hop-adorned bar, the very heart of the hotel, and had apparently been the historical meeting-place of the Hawkhurst Gang two hundred years ago, with a famously gigantic, oversized open fireplace constructed from black ships' beams, covered in ferocious-looking hauberks and spears.

Today a huge fire was burning merrily in the grate.

Posie knew that Richard had decided to cloister himself

in there, with Rufus, and to interview every single guest staying at the hotel. One by one, methodically.

It seemed to be the only plan he had at present.

Monsieur Redon, he of the fish and chips and the intercepted, slightly cryptic French telegrams, was still out, and now regarded as "missing".

Several of the Rye policemen were grouped about the various entrances and exits of the hotel, and it was to be hoped that the Frenchman would be intercepted before long.

Posie lit her Penhaligon's bluebell travel candle, then threw off her shoes, sat atop the ancient, dark-wooden four-poster bed and spread the *Sussex Express* out, open on the page she had been indicated.

It was mainly a farming and agricultural paper, Posie saw that now, but it served too as a sort of round-up of tit-bits of local news, and contained many adverts for Christmas gifts.

This copy was, as Mrs Joab had pointed out, Wednesday's edition, from two days previously, the 2nd December.

Under a large advertisement for 'Electrical Lighting' and sandwiched between another advert for a shop selling dancing shoes for all ages, Posie found her story.

She read it through once, then at least twice more.

LOCAL DANCER MISSING

We are sorry to report what must surely be the end of this unfortunate tale.

Mrs Rosa Rossoli, widow of the late Mr Benito Rossoli (both, in their time, much-loved dancers employed at the Mermaid Hotel in Rye, and lately, at The George, also in Rye) was reported missing by Mr Reginald Spencer, Proprietor of

The George on Saturday 28th November, after she had failed to turn up to work for her regular four o'clock teaching hour.

'This was most uncharacteristic of her,' Mr Spencer is quoted as saying, 'as she loved to dance more than anything else on earth.'

Mrs Rossoli was last seen attending a service at St Mary's Church in Rye on the morning of Friday 27th November, a service to commemorate the life of Queen Alexandra, whose funeral was taking place in London at the same time.

Mrs Rossoli was last seen wearing a purple woollen coat, a purple sequined headscarf in the 'turban' style and carrying a purple umbrella in lieu of a walking stick. All of these were her 'trademark' clothes, such as she wore every day, and which she was well-known around the town for.

Today Inspector George Vallance confirmed that a purple umbrella, much torn and bedraggled, and a single buckled purple dance-shoe, were found swept in among the mud of the Rye Estuary last night by two local fishermen. These items have since been confirmed as being owned by Mrs Rossoli.

Inspector Vallance issued this statement to us today:

'It is my sad duty to inform you that one of Rye's most beloved and easily distinguishable local "characters", Rosa Rossoli, appears to have lost her life through misadventure, probably while walking late at night by the quayside. It seems likely she has drowned, either by accident or design, and whilst there is no body, a death certificate will be drawn up immediately as if a body had been found; the evidence of the wet, ruined clothes is too strong to suggest any other answer to the riddle of where Mrs Rossoli has got to. Any further queries should be addressed to myself at Rye Police Station, or to Mr Bernard Putebank, junior solicitor at Melville & Sons, Rye High Street, who is dealing with Mrs Rossoli's legal estate.'

Posie stretched herself full-length on the bed, and stared up at the lace four-poster canopy ruched high above her.

Not a single thought or emotion seemed to enter her head, which was odd, as her heart was hammering in her chest like a thundering steam train going full pelt.

So her mother was dead.

Gone.

Well, Rosa Parker – *or Rosa Rossoli, as she had become* – had been gone for Posie for a very long time already.

Gone since 1903, in fact.

Therefore, nothing had really changed by learning this news. Although it seemed that Posie had stepped in right at the end of a life which had ended in tragedy.

And yet Posie still didn't seem to feel anything. Just a peculiar numbness. Why was that? *Not even a smidgen of surprise.*

Perhaps she felt a slight stab of disappointment. Because she'd managed to get here, to Rye, to the Mermaid after all.

But it was too late. She was one week too late, if the last sighting of Rosa had been the previous Friday, at church.

Patsy whimpered in her makeshift dog basket by the fire, and a floorboard creaked over near the door.

'You need a walk, don't you, darling?' called Posie lazily from the bed.

Patsy jumped up and began to bark, over and over again. But Patsy didn't come to Posie, as she did usually at the mention of a "walk", but ran instead to the wall, to the panelling, where she got herself into a frenzy, almost hurling herself at the wood.

Posie yawned, stretched. 'Coming.'

The last thing she felt like doing actually was going for a walk, but Patsy's needs were pressing.

Posie put her damp London shoes back on, buttoned up her coat, and jammed her matching cloche hat on her head. She felt she might be a bit insubstantially dressed, and fished hopefully about in her duffle bag under the unread Gamages toy catalogue to see if there was anything else warm to wear, which she might have packed in her earlier hurry and forgotten about.

But there was nothing.

'Perhaps I'll treat myself to a new warm scarf somewhere,' she muttered, grabbing up her purse and Patsy's lead.

And then, as she bent to loop the lead on, Posie felt that pin-prickly sensation of the hairs standing up on the back of her neck which usually accompanied the near-certain knowledge that she was being watched, observed.

Posie snapped up, looked around quickly, but there was nothing.

Behind her, on her bedside table the travel candle had blown out suddenly, and smoke was guttering, spiralling upwards.

A blip of silver seeming to melt away into the wood caught her eye as she spun about but she saw now that there was one of the hotel's regular baubles, this one in silver, hanging in a corner, swaying slightly.

'This place is getting to me,' she whispered to herself.

Posie closed the door hurriedly, locked it. It was only then that she noticed the room's name above the lintel. It read 'KINGSMILL ROOM'.

'Hah!' Posie exclaimed, staring at it. She knew it was one of the hotel's best rooms, and that the placing of her and Richard in it must surely be a coincidence. She knew too that the hotel used the names of some of its more colourful past guests for the names of its rooms, and it had been at least slightly likely that they would have been placed here.

But still.

Thomas Kingsmill, from the brief report Posie had read of him, was not a character she would ever have liked to come across two hundred years ago. A thoroughly despicable man, actually. So what sort of an idiot in this current day and age would hide behind that kind of devilish historical identity in order to meet someone? Whether for genuine purposes, or even in setting a trap?

'Well,' Posie muttered, pocketing the golden room key, and addressing the door, which she knew was stupid, but still: 'Thomas Kingsmill, whoever you are, you can bally well get stuffed. It's going to take something more than you to break a spirit like mine. Or Rufus, for that matter.'

Turning, she saw herself reflected in another huge navy bauble on the landing. She saw large anxious eyes beneath the cloche hat; the fashionable new lipstick which was much too red, even for winter. *Too late to change that now.*

She headed downstairs, past the beams, the jewel-like stained glass everywhere, the feeling of being watched by a thousand interested eyes. Past Mrs Joab at the reception, who was busy sorting out tiny garlands of cream-coloured Christmas lights and polishing up a set of glass angels, while also taking a booking on the telephone.

Posie heaved open the front door, stood for a minute on the step, while Patsy did a jig of fright at the sudden cold beneath her feet. Opposite was 'The House with Two Front Doors' and the huge white-moustached man, the policeman, was still there, looking left and right beneath his jutting cap.

Poor fella, out here in the snow, Posie thought.

Trying his best to help Scotland Yard out on a 'big case'. Doing the job he should have entrusted to one of his Constables.

He was obviously still looking for this Frenchman, Redon, or for any sign of trouble.

Trouble which may or may not be coming.

But Posie saw the policeman had been well-provided for. He had a thermos of something nestled at his feet, and he was drinking a steaming beverage from a porcelain cup which Posie recognised as coming from the hotel; white with a gold mermaid in silhouette on its handle.

She remembered quickly that the man playing sentry was, in fact, a Police Inspector.

Hadn't Richard mentioned him by name?

Inspector Vallance?

And in her mind Posie was scanning the newspaper she had just been reading upstairs. Hadn't Inspector Vallance been the man who had made the statement to the *Sussex Express* about her mother's disappearance, two days ago? He'd had conduct of the case, hadn't he?

Perhaps Posie should talk to him?

The half of her which was ruled by her heart wanted to, and the other, very sensible half, ruled by her head, told herself there was absolutely nothing to talk about here.

Rosa's death had been a tragedy, not a mystery.

There was nothing in the slightest which was suspicious about it.

But the heart won. Of course.

It always did.

She blew out her cheeks in the cold air. It was now or never, so it had to be now.

Posie tripped across the street, hoping the big man didn't notice poor Patsy relieving herself with gusto near his foot, on the snowy cobbles.

'Inspector Vallance?'

The man looked confused, then slightly affronted, then he seemed to recognise Posie from earlier. He drew himself up with as much dignity as one can while wearing a sou'wester.

'Mrs Lovelace, isn't it?'

Posie gulped. She'd made a point of never going by Richard's name. *Ever*. But need's must. 'Er...well, yes, that's right. I wondered if you could help me out, Inspector?'

'Delighted to, Mrs Lovelace. Only I've told your very good husband I won't leave my position here for all the tea in China. So, we'll have to speak here.'

Posie felt that spine-tingling sensation again; a feeling of being watched from the hotel.

She turned abruptly, but there was no-one there; only the panes of mullioned glass windows, glittering in the weak afternoon light.

A clock nearby was striking two o'clock.

She turned back to the Inspector, smiled. 'I saw you were in charge of the Rosa Rossoli case, sir.'

The man harrumphed. 'Hardly a "case", Mrs Lovelace. More like a blip; a sort of non-incident.'

Posie nodded, suddenly feeling a terrible sensation of sadness rush over her. But she hurried on. 'I saw Mrs Rossoli had been declared dead; a certificate drawn up. I just wondered if there was anything unusual about the, er, the non-incident at all?'

Inspector Vallance was looking uncomfortable now. 'Here, you're not some sort of relation, are you, Mrs Lovelace? Because now I think about it, you *do* look very similar to Mrs Rossoli, but I had no idea there was any other family.' He frowned, worried. 'There's the daughter, of course. Miss Dulcie Rossoli.'

'Oh, no, I'm not like Dulcie,' Posie rushed on, defensively, slightly wildly. 'I'm not another daughter! Not close family at all! Rosa Rossoli was a cousin once removed on my mother's side. But you're right; people have always remarked on the family likeness.'

The lies tasted like sawdust in Posie's mouth, but she couldn't go around sharing the truth now, could she?

The Inspector seemed relieved.

'Sad thing; very sad,' he remarked, taking a sip of coffee. 'An unlucky accident, I suppose. But I shouldn't have thought there was much for *you* to worry about, Madam. Nor your good husband. As far as I'm aware there was nothing "unusual" about it at all.'

He paused for a few seconds, then shrugged. 'Oh, except Reggie Spencer, the owner of The George, when he confirmed the shoe which was washed in was hers, he said there was no way Mrs Rossoli would have been wearing that particular purple shoe outside on the quayside. It was a dancing shoe, fancy, see? And worn pretty thin on the sole, come to that. Reggie said Mrs Rossoli always kept her outside street shoes and her dancing shoes separate: he said she was particular. He was adamant there was no way she'd have walked around town in dancing shoes, especially given the cold snap we've been having recently. But he confirmed the washed-in shoe *was* hers, and that was enough for us.'

Posie bit at her lip. 'I see.'

It certainly didn't seem much of an anomaly.

And, as the Inspector was no doubt being kind enough not to point out, the drowning could have actually not been an accident at all, but a suicide.

And, if that had been the case, and Rosa had been desperately unhappy, or not quite in her right mind, who knew what sort of actions she might have taken? Or been capable of? Wearing dancing shoes out in the snowy streets by the quayside might have been the least of Rosa's worries.

Who knew?

'Thank you, Inspector, you've been most kind. I hope this French fella arrives soon for you. You'll catch your death of cold out here otherwise.'

'Mnnn. Oh, Mrs Lovelace, if you're interested, you could do worse than call in on Mrs Rossoli's solicitor, Mr Putebank. He's down on the High Street. Easy to find. You might need to make an appointment though, as he's always very busy: he charges very little and consequently has a good trade, you see.'

'Thank you.'

Posie waved and walked off, crunching her way carefully through the street, battling through the snow. But she didn't head to the High Street immediately; she walked downhill, down Mermaid Street as it curled to where the sea had once washed in, where huge boats had once docked at a harbour which was no longer there, where smugglers had lived and breathed the thrill of contraband.

She passed the Old Borough Arms, where several hardy

sorts sat on wooden benches eating late fish and chips in front of the quayside, a tidal sort of canal in which fishing boats and small tourist boats were currently languishing on mudflats.

This was all that was left of the town's once busy sea trade.

Somewhere here, Posie realised, her mother's clothes had washed in, and conclusions had been formed, decided upon, by the police.

She stood, in the still-dancing snow, looking out at all the bleakness. It seemed like the very edge of the world.

In fact, it reminded Posie very much of Blakeney, where she had been sent to recuperate, up in Norfolk, not that long ago.

Norfolk had been the place of Posie's childhood, a place of rare and raw beauty, much beloved by her father, but hated by her mother.

The gorgeous, wilful, dark-haired Rosa Parker had spent most of Posie's childhood escaping her reality and seeking comfort in the tea-dances which were her passion.

There had been constant trips made by Rosa down to London for all-important dance competitions, followed by strings of missed trains and hastily sent telegrams to Norfolk extending her stays down in the capital.

Sometimes Rosa Parker had been gone for weeks.

A dreadful annual summer holiday to Broadstairs in the year of 1903 had ended badly, and Rosa had left permanently later that same year.

It had been a betrayal from which Posie had, she realised now, never really recovered. It had been bad behaviour, inexcusable.

Posie couldn't imagine walking out on any of her children. Never.

Had life in Norfolk, with the Parker family, really been so bad?

How ironic that this place Rosa had chosen to start a

new life in, with a new husband, and later, a new daughter, should look so much like the place she had fled from!

Posie stared out at the far-off sea. Had Rosa been happy here? Had she run from her new husband, here, too? Caught the train up to London?

And more recently, had she known Posie was there, up in London? Not so far from here? Forging a life for herself, against all the odds?

Had Rosa never once wondered what had happened to Posie?

If she had sunk, or swum?

Posie realised, suddenly, and to her horror, that tears were coursing down her cheeks.

A mother is a mother, after all.

An absent mother, and a dead mother, is still a mother.

What on earth had happened here? Posie dried her eyes on her woollen sleeve and called up a sudden resolve to find answers.

A blip, a sort of non-incident...

No-one deserved to be described like that, did they?

Surely her mother's life – however pitifully she had treated Posie – had been worth more than that? And Rosa's death deserved attention, too.

And, just like that, Posie resolved she would investigate.

****

PART THREE

The Woman in the Purple Dancing Shoes, Thomas Kingsmill and the Plot to get to France

Seven

Posie drank good, strong coffee in the Assembly Rooms of The George.

She had trudged around town, getting colder and colder, and had bought herself a new pair of sheepskin-lined winter boots which she was already sporting, and an enormous turquoise velvet cape, which she was also wearing, despite sitting inside.

Patsy had been treated to a brand-new dog's coat in a festive red tartan, and hadn't protested about having it on. In truth, Posie was now killing time.

She'd called on the solicitor at his small and shabby office at the very end of the High Street, but she'd been told by his equally unprepossessing secretary that Mr Putebank was busy with clients, and could she come back in half an hour, at three o'clock?

So Posie sat waiting, passing time, and the wide-open space of the dance floor with its cluster of tables round the edges, as seen through the windows earlier, had seemed an obvious choice.

She'd spotted the man she guessed had been her mother's boss, Mr Reginald Spencer, scurrying about the place, but she hadn't introduced herself.

What could he possibly add to the sorry tale?

She looked about instead at the place her mother had worked at for the last couple of years, where Rosa had, probably, been happy.

Posie half-watched the women in their gaily-coloured dresses flit before her; saw a dancing teacher, a middle-aged cockney sparrow of a woman with too-orange shingled hair.

The teacher was beating time to the music with a black wooden stick, hitting the floor hard and yelling: 'An' a one, toow, free, and a one, toow, free! That's it, ladies! You got it vewwy nice now! *Vewwy* nice!'

Was this a replacement teacher for Rosa? Or one on a rotation of a set of teachers?

Posie saw that the woman with the orange hair was wearing dancing shoes of a lurid orange suedette, and she frowned, thinking of shoes.

Had Rosa really been scatty enough to walk out in the snow with shoes such as this teacher was wearing? To have gone out into the cold on either Friday 27th November, the day she was last seen, or on Saturday 28th, the day she was reported as missing, in completely unsuitable footwear?

But then, her mother, or what Posie could remember of her, had never been practical, or concerned with the 'right' sort of clothes for the weather.

Unless she had changed in all these intervening years?

There was only one person to ask, and that person was Dulcie. Rosa's other daughter.

Dulcie had crossed Posie's path only once, quite by accident, almost exactly two years previously, when she'd been a guest at a Christmas house party held at Rebburn Abbey, the Cardigeons' stately Yorkshire home.

Dulcie had, at the time, made an unfortunate marriage to a cad and a bounder, but that was all in the past.

A divorce had followed, and freedom of a kind.

Dulcie, at least ten years younger than Posie and bewitchingly beautiful in a very dark, exotic way, had small sparkling brown eyes which seemed to promise the delights of foreign lands and the glimmer of adventure.

It had been Dulcie who had provided Posie with the 'lead': had told Posie that she knew where Rosa Parker had ended up.

She'd informed Posie of Rosa's new 'second' family. Had told Posie that she, Dulcie, was Rosa's daughter by an Italian dancer, and had claimed that she and Posie were related. Dulcie had shown Posie a photograph of her mother, *their* mother, and then Posie had been left in no doubt as to the truth of the girl's excited, excitable claims.

Posie's sister.

A sister who didn't look at all like Rosa, or Posie, but a sister nonetheless.

And even though Posie had never followed up the lead, she had stayed in touch with Dulcie.

She'd heard from Dulcie several times since the stay at Rebburn Abbey: there had been newsy Christmas cards sent to the office; a postcard from Eccles and another from Blackpool. A recent one from South Shields. Posie had written back politely to the addresses which had been given.

This summer a postcard had arrived from Cromer, in Norfolk, of all places, where Dulcie informed Posie she was working in the Hotel de Paris as a professional dancer.

Like mother, like daughter.

Well, not like Posie. Posie couldn't dance for toffee. She took after her father like that, she supposed. She had two left feet.

It had crossed Posie's mind to visit Dulcie at her hotel in Cromer, just along the coast from Blakeney, when she'd been recuperating up in Norfolk a couple of months ago, but it hadn't happened.

In the event, Posie had wanted to get home to Richard and the children with all due speed, was desperate to return to her own, normal life. Besides, the effort of getting to know her 'new' sister all seemed too, too painful on top of other, more recent pain. The discovery of a whole other family seemed too much to deal with.

The timing was wrong.

And it hadn't ever been her mother who had written, only Dulcie.

And that stung.

Posie checked her watch now, and seeing it was almost three o'clock, she drank her coffee quickly, gathered up her belongings and her dog.

The High Street outside was already darkening, and the strings of lights looked magically festive, twinkling amid the snow. She was about to cross the road when someone shouted: 'Miss Parker! Hey, Miss!'

It was Sergeant Fox, satchel swinging, scarf furry-thick with fresh snow.

He was panting and he skidded along the pavement in his hurry to get to her. 'Oh, thank the Lord I found you!'

Her stomach contracted. *Was it Richard?* Had something happened to him? Was the threat to Rufus real, after all? Had Thomas Kingsmill, whoever he was, turned up? Was there actually news of Dolly?

'Don't worry, Miss. Everything's fine. The boss panicked when he realised you'd gone. He thought you were up in your room, dozing or something. Went wild when Mrs Joab said you'd left. He's had me and another Rye policeman stomping about trying to find you.'

'I'm fine.'

Fox looked relieved. He took out a packet of Players and lit himself one, making a shelter against the wind with his big scarf. Taking a deep drag, he raised a blonde eyebrow and looked more like his old cocksure self.

'You've missed us interviewing the entire lot of hotel guests, Miss. There's nothing doing with any of them. Waste of time.'

'The Frenchman? Monsieur Redon?'

Fox took another puff. 'Oh, yes; *him*. Fella's come back, and is probably being put through his paces right now, but from what I saw of him I think it's unlikely he's a criminal mastermind, or even working for one. He's like a short, tubby teddy-bear, ginger and bearded. In his late forties, I'd guess. The fella looked gentle to me, like a music teacher on his holidays. Bumbling, at best.'

This was as close to saying that his boss, Richard, was wrong, as Fox was ever likely to get.

'My instructions were to stick with you, Miss. Like the proverbial sticky stuff. Once I found you.'

'How thrilling for us both.'

'Yep. So where we heading?'

As they crossed the road for the law firm of Melville & Sons, Fox told Posie, between drags on his smoke, that he'd had some joy in finding out who had sent the two curious telegrams for Rufus at one o'clock the day before, the messages telling him to come down to Rye, telling him to bring Posie.

'Our mysterious Mr Thomas Kingsmill, sender of the telegrams, is apparently a fairly young fella,' said Fox, stubbing out his cigarette on the coconut floor mat outside the solicitor's office.

'The lady in the Post Office who dealt with him thought he was in his early twenties; dark, a dashing sort, apparently. "Dapper", she said. He had black hair and sideburns, and a fashionable waxed moustache. Slim and short. He was wearing a three-piece suit in a brown, fancy, patterned material. Had a slight accent…'

None of this sounded good.

'You mean a *foreign* accent, Sergeant?'

'Could have been, yes. The Post Office woman didn't know. But the fella definitely wasn't from these parts. He only said a few words though, so it was difficult for her to be sure. He handed her the words he wanted her to use in the telegrams already written down, see?'

‘Has anyone been seen matching that same description at the Mermaid, Sergeant?’

‘No. Not that I know of. What we doing here, Miss, anyhow? Who on earth are “Melville & Sons”?’

‘Never you mind. And don’t tell Richard.’

‘Right you are, Miss.’

Inside the solicitor’s office, Posie left Fox in the shabby outside waiting room, where he made a show of needing to telephone to the Mermaid, ostensibly to let Richard Lovelace know his wife was safe.

She left Fox holding onto Patsy’s lead as the legal secretary placed the call, and then Posie was ushered into Mr Putebank’s inner sanctum where she sat down at the big desk.

Posie found herself suddenly opposite a slight, scrawny man in a greasy black suit with shiny patches at the elbows, a man in his very early thirties, but with the hangdog, overworked look of a man much older.

She had been about to give him her ‘false’ married name, when the solicitor crossed his arms and declared in a high, reedy voice: ‘You’re Miss Posie Parker, aren’t you?’

She was taken aback, but there seemed no point in denying it.

She explained about seeing Wednesday’s newspaper story, about Rosa Rossoli’s death, and its mention of the solicitor’s name.

‘So here I am.’

‘I know you’re Rosa’s daughter.’

‘Because I look like her?’

‘Partly.’ The young man smiled. ‘But mainly because she told me about you, too.’

Posie’s heart jumped, hammered violently against her ribcage. *This was completely unexpected.*

‘Oh? What did she say?’

Mr Putebank shrugged helplessly. ‘Nothing very useful for you, I’m afraid. She was my client, not my friend, Miss

Parker. But she was dying. I can tell you that. It was nearly all over for her.'

'*WHAT?*'

This caught Posie unawares, and she felt as if someone were shoving her, hurtling her, in front of a fast-moving train, pulling the ground from under her feet, and that she had no way of fighting back, of finding firm ground.

'Yes, Miss Parker. Rosa had a bad heart, some kind of malfunction. She had only a month or so left, the doctors had told her. She came here to change her Will, which she did. She signed it here, too. All above board.'

Putebank made a show of checking a big desk diary. He stabbed at a page.

'It was Thursday, 26th November. Just over a week ago. Unbelievable, really, isn't it? As is your coming here today. Quite the coincidence. In fact, these were going to be sent out today...'

Putebank stood up, checked a wire basket behind his desk and took out two stamped, sealed envelopes, ready for the post.

One was addressed to Posie, at her Grape Street Bureau address, and the other was to Dulcie Rossoli, at the Hotel de Paris, in Cromer.

He passed Posie's letter across to her. 'Give me the envelope back, would you, Miss Parker? We can steam the stamp off. Needs must, I'm afraid.'

Posie ripped it open as if in a dream.

She read the short, typewritten covering letter, and then the copy of the last Will and Testament of Rosemary 'Rosa' Parker which was enclosed.

'She never married again?' Posie asked, looking up. 'Not to Mr Rossoli? Her name here is still given as "Parker"?'

The solicitor shook his head. 'She didn't marry again, no. She lived as Mr Rossoli's common-law wife. Your father never divorced her. Any second marriage would have been illegal, bigamous. The Rossoli's *pretended*, of course, to the town, that they were married. They were concerned what they looked like; always immaculate, very theatrical. She always in purple, him always in brown…'

Posie read down through the Will.

She saw the bulk of Rosa Parker's estate went to Dulcie Rossoli. A small clause added that Posie Parker, 'my eldest daughter', was to get one travel trunk, given to Rosa by Posie's father, when they were first married. And the contents of the trunk, whose value was specified as being nil, were also for Posie.

'You should tell Mrs Joab to call me if she has any problems,' the solicitor said, fishing in his desk drawer and getting out a small bronze-coloured key.

'She can let you have access to your mother's accommodation at the Mermaid. You can get the trunk. It's there, apparently. By law Rosa's rooms had to be sealed up when the death certificate was drawn up, on Wednesday, and the rooms were to be kept sealed until the Will was proved, which can sometimes take weeks, months even. But because this was all so simple, the Rye Probate Registry stamped and signed off on it today. So here's the key to this mysterious trunk.'

Putebank scrawled something on a sheet of headed letter paper, and passed it across to Posie.

'This says Rosa's accommodation should be opened up for you, and the trunk in question is to be removed by you. It does not mention that you are Rosa Rossoli's daughter, or anything else which might, I perceive, be awkward for you.'

Posie was grateful.

'Thank you. Can I ask how this Will, made last week, differed from the Will she had in place before?'

Putebank shrugged half-heartedly. 'I shouldn't tell you, but it makes no material difference. The entire estate – which only amounts to one hundred pounds – was to go to Dulcie in the first Will. In this second Will *you* are mentioned, as is the trunk, both of which are new insertions, but the main provision remains completely unaltered. All the money goes to Dulcie. I hope you weren't counting on the money, Miss Parker? That you aren't too disappointed?'

Posie didn't know what she was feeling, but it certainly wasn't disappointment over money, that was for sure.

Posie was rich, as far as these things went, and Dulcie, last time she had met her, had not had much to call her own, and so she was wholeheartedly glad that Dulcie would benefit.

A sudden sick feeling flooded through her. 'Oh! Have you actually spoken to Dulcie yet? Does she even *know*?'

'That Rosa Rossoli is dead? Yes, I told her on Wednesday, when the death certificate was drawn up, the day after those items were washed in. I reached her at her Norfolk hotel. She was dreadfully upset, naturally, but said she couldn't come down because of work commitments. It's her busiest time of year. She had a dance competition on Wednesday night, and something else every night. I think she hoped to get down here early next week.'

'I see. I'd better telephone her.'

Putebank shrugged. 'That is your business, of course. Not mine. But one thing I will tell you is this: the newspaper report mentions that your late mother attended a church service on Friday 27th, in the morning, and that was the very last sighting of her.'

'Yes?'

Posie stared intently at the little man, trying to tamp down her nerves, her impatience.

'But Rosa told me last Thursday, when she came to make her Will, that she had an important meeting lined up the next day, on the Friday afternoon; that she was going to be going to Hastings. I don't know if she made it; it sounds very much like she didn't, somehow. That she stayed in Rye, fell in the water...But I thought, well, I just *felt*, you should know.'

‘Thank you.’

Posie put the letter and copy of the Will in her bag, together with the small bronze key she had been handed, and left, together with Fox, who was excitable with fresh news, gleaned on the telephone from Richard.

He carried Patsy under his arm, on top of his satchel, as they trudged along the High Street.

‘No Thomas Kingsmill yet, then, Sergeant?’

‘Nah, Miss. The guests are all confined to their rooms for now, and there’s nothing doing with any of them. Oh, big news, Miss! The French gentleman your husband was so keen to find turns out to be the Mermaid’s wine importer, over on one of his quarterly trips from Epernay, in France.’

Fox shook his head incredulously. ‘He brings over wine direct from his employer, and the Proprietress of the Mermaid chooses what she wants. He sells to other businesses in the town, too. Those telegrams in French were sent back to Epernay. Boring business stuff! It seems a particular champagne is no longer available, and this was a sort of grievance for both sides, which had to be smoothed over. But it beats me why the foreign fella had to send such bally cryptic telegrams to his boss. I *do* realise why your husband was suspicious.’

Posie shrugged, unsurprised at this recent development.

She had always thought Richard had overreacted. ‘Perhaps they weren’t cryptic at all: the world of wine may have its own language, Sergeant?’

Fox was continuing, unfazed: ‘And speaking of *foreign*. The Earl’s Lagonda at Hastings hasn’t been salvaged yet; the police there wonder if it’s even possible. It’s half-stuck in the mud on a very treacherous outcrop where the sea is particularly deep. Divers can’t get to it.’

Fox shook his head dismally, relishing the tale. ‘It’s gone in right off the Hastings cliffs; must have shot off them with some momentum! It looks like it started its descent from near a popular cliff-walk. And there's a woman – who your husband is convinced is Dolly Cardigeon's French pal – who was seen yesterday near the crash-site; well, she's been sighted on the cliffs again, watching the car. All morning.'

Posie frowned. This seemed odd. 'Has anyone questioned her, Sergeant?'

'The Chief Commissioner has asked them to; I haven't heard any more.'

'I doubt if she's anything to do with it; probably just a curious, morbid local, rubbernecking. You get that type everywhere. But the woman should be spoken to, definitely. Perhaps this woman knows something? We desperately need more information about this weird affair, don't we? Because I'm trying to look at the whole picture here, the enticing of Rufus down to Rye, and it doesn't make sense if we try and explain it with the facts we have so far. The timing is all wrong, isn't it?'

'How so, Miss?'

'Well, the car crash *can't* be connected with the young dark man in his patterned brown suit with the unplaceable accent who sent the telegrams to Rufus yesterday. He was *here* in Rye, at the Post Office, just before one o'clock. The Lagonda must have been taken from Rufus' garage in central London at about one-fifteen, I suppose. So whoever stole it, and whoever drove it the two hours to Hastings, then crashed it around three-thirty, as twilight was coming on, certainly wasn't the same fella.'

'Mnnn. Well, the driver of the Lagonda wasn't the French wine importer, either. Monsieur Redon has watertight alibis for all of yesterday, and he was in Rye, all day long, at various hotels and restaurants, plying his wares.'

'Of course he was.'

And then they were back at the Mermaid and Posie was at the reception, asking for Mrs Joab, but being told she wasn't around at present.

Fox lingered behind Posie, leafing casually through his trusty guidebook about ghosts, the dog still tucked under his arm.

Evans tried to be helpful. He scanned the note from Mr Putebank.

'Mrs Rossoli, Madam? You want to access her rooms?'

He looked up in incomprehension, but at Posie's answering silence he opened a drawer and searched frantically.

After a few moments he tugged something from the back of the drawer.

It was an old map.

It was grubby and looked like it had been drawn in pencil, with careful writing and many rubbings-out.

'What's that?' asked Posie, interested.

'It's a map of the whole building, Madam. Includes all the tunnels, and hidey-holes. There are just so many secret ways that one simply can't remember them all. It's impossible. The original map was made by the Hawkhurst Gang, who dug many of the tunnels here themselves. It's been copied since, obviously. Many times over. This is just one of the several we keep here, and even this was made years ago, by the look of things, although it's not one I'm familiar with.'

Evans sighed, looked put-upon. He left the map on the counter, looking through other drawers.

'We normally have a few maps, but I can't put my hands on any others right now, which is odd. Mrs Joab, of course, knows the tunnels and passageways like the back of her hand, but I really don't know where she's disappeared off to: she's supposed to be here until the dinner-time shift! It's a lucky thing I popped back when I did, otherwise we'd be completely unmanned!'

Evans looked flustered, started opening and shutting cupboards rather wildly. 'Anyway, I *had* thought there was a shortcut up to Mrs Rossoli's apartment, so it was worth consulting the map, but perhaps I'm wrong. That map certainly shows nothing of the kind...Now, where is the key?'

He eventually retrieved a key with a bit of string attached and a tatty piece of paper with the number '32' on it.

He handed it to Posie.

She flipped it around in her hand, frowned. The back of the paper read 'CHECK THE PAIRS' and the words had been added in a bright purple ink.

'Excuse me, Mr Evans.' Posie pointed at the text. 'What does that mean? Is there a double of this key? A pair?'

Evans read the paper on the key and shook his head.

'Never seen that note before, Madam. And no, that's our only copy. Mrs Rossoli would have had her own key to her flat with her when she disappeared, Madam. It hasn't been retrieved. And I think, but I can't be certain, that that *is* Mrs Rossoli's handwriting. She always used purple ink, you see? I saw it when she dropped letters off for posting. It's certainly not my writing, or Mrs Joab's. But I'm sure it's nothing important.'

'Thank you.'

'You'd best follow me, Madam. It's a long way; a complicated route right to the top of the building. Only Rosa lived up there, although in the days before the Great War several families who worked here shared the floor, all sharing one bathroom, too. Shall we go?'

And so Posie followed.

As did Sergeant Fox, who ignored Evans' strange looks, and blundered along with Patsy in his arms and his head still in his book, paying heed to Lovelace's command not to let Posie venture off alone.

But Posie saw that actually what Fox was looking at, tucked inside the book, was the grubby map of the Mermaid's layout.

Obviously filched from the desk when Evans hadn't been looking.

* * * *

Eight

The apartment, Number 32, when they got there, was high up at the very back of the building.

Posie entered alone, leaving Fox outside the front door, on the small landing. She told him she wanted privacy.

The entrance was long and dark and narrow, an initial corridor with uneven floorboards which contained a tiny kitchenette built into one side.

This opened out onto a bigger area, split into two rooms, each with one sash window overlooking the rooftops of Rye. A small, neat bedroom with a double bed, and a living-room.

The view from the living-room showed the glitter of the far-off sea in the failing light, but the snow had mounted on the window-sills outside, and the windowpanes were almost covered.

Not much light came in.

The place was immaculate, but it was freezing and smelt musty.

My mother's space.

Posie snapped on the electric light in the living-room.

One old sofa and one small, cheap coffee table were revealed. There was a mirror on the wall with no frame and a vase with fake, purple silk roses in it, now gathering dust.

A line of basic metal pegs were nailed high on the wall next to a small wooden dining table - which had been pushed into a tight corner – and these pegs were hung with a couple of purple coats, none heavy enough for winter.

On the dining table was some reading material: a guidebook about Rye; a book about the Mermaid, open at a chapter; a newspaper, the *Sussex Express*, and a couple of dancing magazines.

There was a Parish magazine, too, for St Mary's Church, left open on the page about the service to commemorate Queen Alexandra.

So far, nothing odd.

The mantlepiece above the boarded-up fireplace held one silver-framed photograph of Dulcie, taken not that long ago, smiling in a tiara and ball-dress, obviously at some dancing event.

Posie pulled her gaze away from it quickly, desperate not to feel jealousy, or *anything*, in fact. She was very much aware that she had not been invited here; that she was encroaching on a personal, safe, sacred space.

It had been up to her mother to decide who she displayed in photographs on the mantelpiece.

It was none of Posie's business.

Get over it.

And then there were a series of small silver cups. Twenty, thirty of them, all highly polished and obviously much treasured. On closer inspection, these were revealed as dancing trophies, won at local competitions, inscribed variously with Benito and Rosa Rossoli's names, and mentioning various years reaching back to 1904.

You did well here, Posie thought. *But you lived meagrely. Lightly*.

And what a small, poky, dark place in which to bring up a child! There hadn't even been a bedroom here for Dulcie, Posie realised suddenly.

She must have had to sleep on the sofa.

But perhaps there had been great happiness here? A happiness which had lasted for more than twenty years.

However, that happiness was absent now, as was its last occupier.

Emptiness, pure and simple, filled the space.

But the flat had a curious feel to it. As if the very rooms themselves were watching Posie; waiting.

There was a sudden creak of a floorboard nearby, and a rattle of a draught came from the fireplace. Then the sudden slamming of a door echoed nearby.

'Fox?' she called out suddenly. 'Sergeant?'

Posie had that pin-prickly feeling again, but it was ridiculous! Completely unwarranted. There weren't even any strange reflective baubles here, on which to blame flickering shadows for giving her the creeps.

Her unease was only in her head.

'I'm still here, Miss.' Fox's voice from outside was calm, level.

'Send Patsy in, will you?'

'Right you are.'

A second later the small dog was skittering along the corridor, jumping at Posie delightedly. And then she was barking madly, as if in anguish, tearing at the walls.

'I know, that's how I feel too, darling dog. Something's not right here, is it? Well, let's find this trunk, eh? And then we can leave.'

The bedroom was different to the living-room. Neat, but full with two cheap cupboards on either side of the bed. A scent of mothballs lingered.

One cupboard was jam-packed with a woman's dancing clothes, lilac and violet and purple silk dresses in a very small size, with feather boas, and belts with twinkling stones glued on, all looped about in a big old mess.

There were hats and wigs, too.

And a huge cardboard box of many pairs of used suedette dancing shoes, in a range of purple hues; many with buttons and sparkly bits glued on, some with fake buckles with rhinestones. Pretty things, but cheap.

One shoe right on the top of the pile had a buckle shaped like a butterfly, worn down badly.

There were probably more than fifteen pairs here. The soles of all of these were worn thin, and they smelt horrid, musty and sweaty, as all old shoes do.

Perhaps they had been prize-winning shoes, Posie thought to herself. Why else would they be kept?

It was like a little girl's dressing-up box of disguises and make-believe.

My father would never have allowed her all this, Posie thought with a half-smile.

He had been a lovely man, the Reverend Parker, but a stick-in-the-mud; conscious of public appearances and his own social standing.

I suppose I'm glad Rosa got what she wanted, in the end. A second chance.

A chance to be truly herself.

The other cupboard was full, too, but this was something of a surprise. This one was full of a man's clothes, and their combined scent of old pomade oil, and sweat, and dust came reeking out at her.

Most of the clothes were also dancing outfits: fancy suits in glitzy, cheap materials, mainly browns with large checks, or intricate raised velvet patterns, or flecked with metallic thread, all made to catch the light of the ballroom.

At the bottom of this cupboard were boxes of stacked-heeled men's dancing shoes, and hats, and wigs, and fake moustaches, fake beards and hair pieces. In all colours.

Another dressing-up box fit for a peacock. A box full of dreams and vivacity, all now gone.

These had obviously been the clothes and belongings of Benito Rossoli.

And suddenly Posie felt like an intruder, like she was overstepping the mark.

She saw there were boxes of photographs, and letters, and diaries, all stacked neatly in Benito's cupboard and the curious part of her wanted to grab at them, go through them. Hunt for the key to the happiness which had been sought here. But she immediately stopped herself.

These are not my things to pry into.

'Come on,' she said to herself. 'Find the trunk.'

It was under the bed.

A neat burgundy travel trunk with expensive wooden inlays, not much bigger than an average suitcase. Posie recognised it as the identical twin to one her father had owned; one she had given away on his death when she'd had to sort through his belongings several years earlier.

She got down on the ground and pulled it out.

It wasn't dusty, and seemed in much better condition than the one her father had had; he'd covered his with travel stickers and old border entry stamps, from the many and various foreign journeys he had made over the years.

This one looked as if it had never left the room, let alone the country. It seemed likely that Rosa had never, once having arrived here, gone away again.

Posie slotted the bronze key which Putebank had given her in the lock of the trunk, and had that strange feeling of being observed again, but turning sharply saw it was only Patsy watching her, bright-eyed, but growling.

'Two minutes, and we'll be gone, darling. I'm not enjoying this much either.'

The lock clicked easily; in fact, Posie would have sworn the thing had been forced at some point, and it eased.

Posie threw back the lid. She sat back on her haunches and stared.

If she had been expecting much, she would have been disappointed. But the truth was that she had been expecting nothing, and so she had nothing to lose.

A chemical-like, library scent of dust and ink rose to greet her.

What she saw, neatly stacked in the case were letters. Blue, thin, Basildon Bond envelopes, most crunchy with age. All of them were covered in the same spiky purple handwriting as on the paper attached to the key to this accommodation. But some letters were much faded.

Posie let a heavy, weary breath escape her.

She put out a hand, brushed it across the stiff envelopes. There must have been hundreds of letters in the trunk, possibly a thousand. She pulled out a letter at random from the left-hand side of the trunk, and felt the missive, crispy with age, weighing nothing in her hand.

It was dated '1904' and was addressed to 'Miss Rosemary Parker, The Vicarage, Holkham, Norfolk'.

Ripping the thing open, Posie saw a couple of thin, matching sheets, covered in spiky purple letters. She saw the words 'darling girl' and 'sorry'.

There were many 'sorrys'.

Posie shoved the letter back inside the old envelope, feeling like she might be sick. She shoved it back in its place.

She went now to the right-hand side of the trunk, where the ink was darker, fresher, and the year on the envelope was marked '1925'.

The letters on this side of the trunk were addressed to 'Miss Posie Parker, Detective' and her Grape Street Bureau address was used. Most of these letters were open, looked like they had never been sealed.

Taking an envelope out at random, Posie saw it was from the summer, for inside was a letter and a cut-out from *The Times* of Posie standing with Rufus outside his house in London, under the headline 'MISSING COUNTESS CAUSES A STIR FOR POSIE'.

Posie stuffed it all back haphazardly.

So she did know where to find me, she thought desperately. 'She knew what I did, and where I worked, and probably where I lived. But why on earth did she never send me these? There must be letters here stretching back over twenty-two years, perhaps one written every week. More than a thousand letters…'

What strange logic had prompted Rosa Rossoli to lock her words – her love? – away like this, rather than communicate it.

It would have made all the difference in the world. Posie brushed an inconvenient tear away.

A door swung, another creak, a draught of wind. Patsy was barking manically now.

There was a sudden knock, the front door opening. It was Fox.

'Miss? We need to go down, Miss. It's urgent. I can hear something downstairs. Can I help you with anything here?'

Slamming the lid of the trunk, Posie hauled it out of the bedroom.

She hoisted it up and gave it to Fox in the dim corridor where the kitchenette was and he almost staggered.

'Let's go. I won't need to come back here, Sergeant.'

But just then she caught sight of a photograph, blurry, taped to the grubby wooden wall above the sink with its two dirty cups.

Posie leant up to look, pressed her body against the warmth of the metal sink.

It was a photograph of Rosa, the only one on display in the entire place; taken perhaps ten, fifteen years before. Before the Great War.

Before our lives changed, while my brother was still alive.

Rosa was standing in front of a tea hut which said 'Ludlam's Teas and Ices', and it had obviously been a blustery day.

Rosa had her hair piled up as Posie remembered, a loose black tendril blowing forwards, her arms around a girl of about ten years old, dark-haired, smiling, immaculate in a pinafore, clutching at a bucket and spade.

The girl was the spitting image of the man at their side,

dark-haired, fancily-dressed, small and neat; every inch a ballroom dancer.

Benito, Dulcie's father.

A happy family.

Something made Posie rip the photo down and take it with her.

Posie felt the weight of the empty flat pressing down on her as she turned for a last time, locked the door behind her, felt an impossible sadness upon her that she wanted to run from.

'What's happening, Sergeant?'

'Dunno, Miss, but I reckon something's going on. I can hear that Inspector Vallance fella hollering downstairs like a champion.'

They were charging back the way they had come. Fox had stuffed the pencil map of the Mermaid and his book back into his satchel and was carrying the trunk like a dead weight.

'You know, there's something funny about that room up there, Miss: Number 32. There isn't a secret passageway to it, not on this map, but I could swear I heard doors, footsteps, almost in the walls themselves.'

'Patsy would agree with you. Some of your famous ghosts, perhaps?'

'Very funny, Miss.'

Down on the ground floor all hell had broken loose. Any attempts to stage an undercover operation had fallen by the wayside, and Inspector Vallance was tearing around the red-painted corridors, men in full uniform now adding to the general panic.

Posie saw Richard standing by reception, smoking one of his Turkish cigarettes as if his life depended on it, his face set, his whole stance one of humiliated anguish.

'Darling?'

'Mnnn?' He seemed barely to take Posie in, nor Sergeant Fox.

'What on earth has happened here, Richard?'

'It's the Earl, Posie. I'd left him for just a moment in the Giant's Fireside Bar, with lads from the Rye Police Force stationed at both the exit into the yard, and the exit into the hallway. He was sampling another whisky, I think. At the bar. But he was certainly all alone. I swear to God I was gone no more than two minutes – I wanted to speak to Mrs Joab, but I couldn't find her – and when I came back, he had gone.'

Richard was frighteningly calm. But he looked more serious than Posie had ever known him. He stubbed his smoke out viciously.

'Rufus never left by either of the exits, the police lads swear it. And he's simply disappeared into thin air.'

* * * *

Nine

Police were crawling over the large, many-levelled building, and alerts had been put out at the train station, on all the main roads leaving Rye, and at the out-of-town harbour, with descriptions of Rufus being handed out left, right and centre.

It would be difficult to find him though, everyone conceded, as it was almost completely dark now.

'But *how* was it possible?' whispered Posie. She stood a little aside, letting the general melee around her go on.

Richard was on the telephone, muttering darkly. Fox had tucked Rosa Rossoli's travel trunk in tight behind the reception desk which was unmanned.

'What is it I'm not seeing here?' Posie spoke aloud. 'Or what is it that I've *seen*, but not understood?'

She looked down into her hand, where the key to apartment 32 was still pressed, and where the photograph she had stolen was slightly crunched up.

She placed both of these on the glass counter.

Fox was studying the pencilled map of the building again, and Evans, the receptionist, suddenly appeared, red-faced and sweating.

'Oh, thank heavens! I've been searching all over for that wretched map! *You've* got it, Sergeant! The police have been asking me about all the hidey-holes. I couldn't help them, and Mrs Joab has vanished! Can you give that map to the Chief Commissioner? He wanted it urgently. Oh, here he is; he's off the telephone!'

Richard was in an uncharacteristically foul temper.

'The deuce! Where is Mrs Joab? She *knew* we had a crucial operation going on here! Hardly the time to go off shopping, or whatever it is she's up to!' growled Lovelace uncharitably, and he snatched the map from Fox and pored over it.

'See here, sir,' said Fox, jabbing his finger at a section marked 'GIANT'S FIRESIDE BAR'.

'There's a Priest's Hole marked here, isn't there? Built into the chimney place, right by the fire?'

'Yes, Evans here mentioned it already. It's well-known but it's a waste of time.'

'I agree it doesn't look hopeful, sir: there's no mention of any connecting passageways on the map, are there? So it could well be simply somewhere to stand and wait for danger to pass. Which may be how someone was able to wait, and then get out and grab the Earl at an opportune moment, when you left him alone, sir? But how would this mysterious person spirit the Earl away? Perhaps we *should* check it out, sir: the Earl could be in there, as we speak, with our mysterious "Thomas Kingsmill".'

Lovelace was shaking his head. 'It's not possible, lad. The Earl and I were in that Bar for almost two hours, and the fire was roaring in the grate all the time. Anyone waiting in the chimney for an opportune moment to grab the Earl would have been fried alive.'

Fox was insistent. 'We *should* look, sir. These routes and hiding-spots were invented by the Hawkhurst Gang, weren't they? And they were ingenious, resourceful fellas by the sound of it. They *had* to be. We should at least check it out, sir.'

Posie was staring at the map, too.

But as if for the very first time, with fresh eyes.

Because she suddenly realised she recognised the writing on the map.

She looked quickly over at the key to room 32, at the purple ink, with its message in the same hand as the letters written over twenty-two years, kept in the immaculate trunk.

'CHECK THE PAIRS.'

Posie saw Richard and Sergeant Fox hurrying off to the Giant's Fireside Bar, followed closely by Evans.

Thoughts were cramming into her mind, running fast, overflowing, her head clearer than it had been in months.

She felt as if she had been swimming, drowning, and she was coming up at last for a gasp of pure, blissful air.

Images skittered through her mind, clear as day.

She recalled Fox's description of the man who had sent Rufus telegrams at the Post Office, the mysterious 'Thomas Kingsmill'; he'd been wearing a three-piece suit in a brown, fancy, patterned material. He'd had black hair and a fashionable moustache; been slim and short. Had a slight accent.

That description could have fitted the man in the photograph she'd left on the reception desk. *Benito Rossoli.*

Rosa's husband.

Could it be possible?

Of course not, because the Italian, Benito Rossoli, had been dead these last two years, but what if…?

And then other thoughts, unconnected but important, flooded Posie's mind: a buckle, shaped like a butterfly; sets of handwriting she knew; a key with an instruction on it; a map of a place filled with ghosts, hoaxes, and too much history, where people were likely to get scared, and believe in the unlikely.

The impossible.

But Posie didn't believe in ghosts.

And in her mind, absolutely everything was possible.

She remembered Richard's words earlier. '*It seems as if the game has changed.*'

Well, yes: it had.

And she was slowly realising what was happening here. But there were gaps, things she still didn't understand.

She marched around the empty desk, and was about to pick up the telephone and speak to the Operator, when Inspector Vallance came chugging in, still wearing his black sou'wester, excitement all over his face.

'They've opened up the Priest's Hole, Mrs Lovelace. And it seems it was a clever little bit of Hawkhurst gang engineering, all sealed up against the heat! Unbelievable. And they've found the Earl's hip-flask in there, together with a lot of spilled whisky and a smashed glass. Seems he was forced in there against his will!'

Posie nodded slowly.

Yes, that made sense.

'But they haven't actually found Rufus?'

Vallance looked suddenly resigned, less elated. 'No, Mrs Lovelace. There are about six tunnels all leading off from there,' he said. 'And they all look dangerous; haven't been used in years. Your husband is waiting for Mrs Joab to return, to tell him which route leads where, and if any of the tunnels are safe.'

She isn't going to return.

Posie was about to voice this unwelcome thought when she saw Inspector Vallance holding up the photograph she'd taken from Rosa's apartment.

He looked over at Posie, frowning. 'This yours, Madam? That's Mrs Rossoli there, isn't it? With her family? Oh, jeepers, that's a bit odd.'

'What's odd, Inspector?'

Vallance stabbed a thick, stubby finger at something in the background of the snapshot. 'See this place, Ludlam's? The café here?'

'Yes. What of it?'

'It's in Hastings. In exactly the spot where our Hastings colleagues are busy working tonight. Well, they are working *below* it, to be accurate. It's a popular tourist spot, high on the cliffs. Although Ludlam's is closed up, of course, in the wintertime. It's where that priceless Lagonda of Earl Cardigeon's flew over the cliff yesterday into the sea.'

Valance sighed heavily. 'And we've had problems at Ludlam's itself this past week, too; reports of some sort of vermin or foxes there, in the bins at the back, although no-one has investigated it so far; what with all the snow. And it's not a priority, either. The place is all bolted shut.'

He handed the photograph to Posie with a smile.

'Some interest you've got there, Mrs Lovelace, for a cousin-once-removed, eh?'

Posie ignored him. 'When did these disturbances at the café start up?'

The Inspector shrugged, losing interest. 'Oh, I dunno. Saturday, just gone? Sunday, maybe? Around the same time we had reports of a woman in purple clothes hanging around the place. This foreign lass. I hear she's been seen there again, yesterday and today. Probably some busybody…'

This was the woman Richard had thought might be Violette, the French woman involved in Dolly's disappearance.

Funny clothes.

Purple.

This detail, calling to mind so instantly her mother in her final incarnation as a dancing teacher in Rye, was painful for Posie.

The purple clothes hadn't been mentioned before. Neither had the fact that the woman had been seen before yesterday.

Lovelace and Fox were back, speaking in low, wretched, animated whispers.

Evans lurked about, looking like he might cry.

'Could I ask for your help, Mr Evans?' Posie asked, falsely cheery. 'Do you keep a log of staff telephone calls? I'm wondering if Mrs Rossoli made a call from here last week, perhaps on Wednesday or Thursday? Could you find out for me? And *where* exactly she called?'

'Of course, Madam.'

Evans started to flick through a neat green leather ledger behind the desk, happy to be able to do something constructive.

Richard came over, brows furrowed. 'Mrs Rossoli? What the deuce, Posie love? What's she got to do with this mess?'

It's complicated. Just like my mother was in real life.

But Evans had found what he needed. He stabbed at an entry jubilantly.

'It was Wednesday night, last week, Madam. Wednesday 25th November. Mrs Rossoli made a call, two minutes in length. Same number Rosa always called; every week. Although Wednesday wasn't her usual day. She normally called once a week, on a Sunday evening.'

He said a name, a place, and the policemen in the room stared, mystified.

But this all made sense to Posie.

Finally, the gaps were closing.

'I wonder, Mr Evans, can you help again? Can you call the same number, now? Can you ask them if a man who lives there is currently missing?'

Evans gulped. 'What name shall I give, Madam? For this missing man?'

Posie felt like laughing suddenly, hysterically. She passed the photograph of the cliff at Hastings to Evans, who recoiled slightly.

'Describe the man in that photograph to them,' she said lightly, tapping the image of her mother's Italian lover.

'But he's dead, Madam!' wailed the receptionist. 'I used to know him; he lived here. That was Benito Rossoli!'

'Well, that remains to be seen,' said Posie crisply. 'Now, please hurry.'

And then she turned to Sergeant Fox, who looked at her full on, excitement dancing in his light eyes. *He knows the game is on now*, thought Posie.

He'll help me.

She grabbed the key to room 32 again, with the note: 'CHECK THE PAIRS.'

It seemed her mother was being practical, useful, helpful to her at the last.

She shoved the key into Sergeant Fox's hands. 'I can't face going back to those rooms again, Sergeant. But you will, won't you?'

'Of course, Miss, what am I looking for?'

'In the bedroom, in one of the cupboards, is some women's clothing. At the bottom of the cupboard is a box of purple dancing shoes. Grab the whole box, bring it down here. And while you're there, check the sink, will you?'

'What for?'

'Anything. Anything at all.'

She turned to Inspector Vallance. 'Sir, could you get one of your constables to go to your police station, to the exhibits section. I need all of the effects from the drowning of Rosa Rossoli.'

The Inspector raised his shaggy eyebrows in surprise, almost indignation, but Richard, angrily uptight at not having a clue what was unravelling before him, chivvied the man on: 'Go on, Inspector. Do as my wife says: it could be life or death for the Earl.'

And suddenly Posie and Richard were alone at last, with just Evans telephoning in the corner.

Richard cupped Posie's face in his huge right hand, stroked her cheek gently with his thumb.

'What the blazes is all this about, darling? *Rossoli*? Are you sure? And what about Rufus? Do you know where he is, to boot?'

'I think so, yes. Yes: I do.'

'By Gad, you've done well here. Better than all of us. Is he out on the marshes, on his way to France already?'

'I think not, darling. He's somewhere far colder. A dreadful place, in fact.'

* * * *

Ten

'Here they are, Miss,' said Fox, putting the box of shoes on the red carpet of reception.

Posie squatted down.

Check the pairs.

Twelve pairs, thirteen pairs, fourteen...

No.

Thirteen pairs, and one single shoe; a left shoe, with no matching partner.

A purple shoe, almost worn out, with a fancy sparkly buckle in the shape of a butterfly as its decoration. Posie nodded to herself. She had been right. An anomaly.

She'd checked the pairs.

She stood up, clutching the single shoe.

It felt small, delicate, in her hand. Insubstantial.

Lovelace was looking at her, scowling very slightly. He didn't speak.

'And the sink, Sergeant?'

'Nothing in the sink, Miss. Strange funny noises though; a clanking of pipes and all that.'

Posie nodded. 'That's what I expected you to say.'

Evans came off the telephone. He was excited, buzzing. He stabbed at the photograph Posie had left on the counter.

'A gentleman answering to this description, going by

the name of Nicky Carter, has gone missing, Madam. A dashing sort, originally from Tyneside. He left the place I just called last Friday morning, Madam, very early. Hasn't been back.'

'Sounds about right. Hmmm, Tyneside, eh? That would account for a 'foreign accent' I suppose…'

'Who is this fella, Posie love?' cut in Richard Lovelace hurriedly. 'Is he our man?'

But just at that moment, Inspector Vallance and a young policeman in uniform came rushing in, holding a large brown paper bag, marked 'EVIDENCE'.

The young man was panting, dusted in snow, but he ripped open the bag and shook the contents onto the floor.

Posie picked over two sad objects, barely recognisable for what they were.

A slimy, mud-encrusted dress umbrella, and a poor, mangy bit of leather, mud-caked, hardly like a shoe at all.

But she picked it up, held it aloft with a kind of pride.

Through the mud sparkled a butterfly-shaped buckle. And the shoe was a right one.

'No wonder you thought Rosa Rossoli had drowned, Inspector,' Posie said, turning to Inspector Vallance. She silently reunited the two shoes together, holding one in each hand, as a matching – but not quite matching – pair. She showed them all around, to general consternation and puzzlement.

Posie kept her voice firm, kept it from wavering: 'But the truth is that Rosa Rossoli didn't drown here in Rye, and she certainly never wore these shoes to go out walking in. Mainly because she was silly and sentimental and she treasured them. She would have hated to see this shoe in this state.'

She turned to her husband.

'Let's go and get Rufus, Richard,' she said quickly. 'Do you happen to have a gun?'

'A gun?' hissed Lovelace. 'Well, as a matter of fact…'

'You'd better bring it along, darling. And get some more men to guard that Priest's Hole again. Oh, and bring that old map up, will you, Sergeant?'

****

The rooms which comprised apartment '32' upstairs were as cold and uninviting as before.

Lovelace went first, reluctantly wielding a small service pistol, with Fox shouldering along behind him. Posie followed, carrying Patsy, and Inspector Vallance brought up the rear.

She'd hoped never to set foot in this place again, but, as sometimes happened, things had come together and she'd understood everything, at last.

Understood the awful, shallow, silly, pathetic, cheap truth of this case.

They all stood about in the bare electric light, and slowly the men turned to Posie, waiting, the atmosphere tense.

Posie spoke clearly, each word spelled out loudly.

'This is a strange little case in which things are very much not as they seem. The Chief Commissioner was right earlier when he said that he felt as if the game had changed once we arrived here, and that's because it *had*. Because what on the surface looked like one thing, was really quite another. We thought initially that this was a plot to ensnare the Earl of Cardigeon, which, eventually, it did turn into. But really, the Earl was simply the bait. Bait to get *me* here, and trap me, probably to kill me. And all of this was just the icing on the cake of a full-blown murder which had already occurred. A murder which has gone unnoticed so far, and unavenged...'

'*What*?' said Richard, gobsmacked.

Posie motioned around herself.

'This was the apartment in which my own estranged mother lived, for the last twenty-or-so years. With her beloved common-law Italian husband, Benito, and with her very much beloved daughter, Dulcie.'

Richard was still holding the gun, eyes fixed on Posie, biting at his lip, but not interrupting.

She carried on: 'Rosa Rossoli won several dancing competitions, and while the prizes were not huge, they mounted up. In the last few years she'd managed to save around one hundred pounds for her daughter, Dulcie, who was also a talented dancer.'

Posie tried not to let a tremor enter her voice.

Go on.

'A daughter who had gone through a bad marriage and might need that money someday, to get back on her feet. But, as it turned out, this bit of money was the absolute undoing of everyone. Especially of Rosa.'

Posie sat down on the shabby sofa. She held a trembling Patsy on her lap and hugged her quiet.

'Rosa was dying. She'd been told she didn't have long to live, and she'd started to get her affairs in order. She altered her Will to include a gift for *me*, as it happens. But there began a stupid misunderstanding.'

Posie explained that things had gone wrong, spiralled hideously out of control.

'Evans confirmed, just now, that last Wednesday Rosa called the Hotel de Paris, in Cromer, where my half-sister Dulcie worked. I'm guessing this bit, but I think Rosa wanted to tell Dulcie that she was going to change her Will on the Thursday, and that this new Will would include *me*. I don't think Rosa meant to taunt Dulcie, but perhaps she conveyed her message to her in a deliberately uncertain way, in order to get Dulcie to come and visit. Maybe she made it sound as if she was leaving me all of the money, or that she was splitting it in half?'

Posie shrugged. 'Perhaps Rosa was lonely, and wanted a visit from her far-away daughter, ever busy with a career which seemed to include no time for Rosa at all. Particularly as Dulcie now had a new beau who was taking up all of her free time…'

'What of it, darling?'

Posie could sense Richard's impatience, his worry seeping into the horrible cold sitting-room.

'Well, Rosa's telephone message worked. Dulcie, my sister, promised to meet my mother on Friday last week, in the afternoon. To discuss things. Rosa told Mr Putebank she was meeting someone at Hastings, and I'm pretty sure this was Dulcie. I think they met at an old and favourite spot of theirs, on the cliff-top; Ludlam's Teas and Ices, even though it was closed. Rosa must have gone there about lunchtime, after church. And I don't know what happened, but something went very, very wrong.'

Posie took a deep breath.

'I think there must have been a conversation about the altered Will, perhaps with my share still being left deliberately vague by Rosa, and then there was an argument by the closed-up café. A scuffle? Perhaps it was also about Dulcie's new fella, who had accompanied her down from the Hotel de Paris in Cromer that day, where they both worked. His name, by the way, is Nicky Carter. And he is a fellow dancer; a ringer for Dulcie's own deceased father. But I think I am right when I say that he is a wrong'un; and I think that Rosa saw that last week. Maybe she said as much. Anger and resentment flowed over, and I don't know if it was meant to happen, but somehow Rosa Rossoli – my mother – died that day.'

Inspector Vallance gasped. 'Madam, are you sure?'

Posie shrugged.

'I'm not sure, no, Inspector. And I have no evidence for this part of the story. But it seems more than likely. I reckon Dulcie and Nicky buried Rosa where they had been sitting, perhaps at the back of that freezing café? But they didn't bury her deep enough. You said there were reports of animals, disturbances?'

'Makes sense.' Vallance nodded, looking grim. 'And the woman in purple, that was your sister, Miss Dulcie?'

'Perhaps.' Posie hurried on.

'I think Dulcie returned with all due haste to her place of work, to Cromer, so it looked as if she had had nothing to do with her mother's death, just in case the body was discovered. But the pair were lucky, the snow which started up a day or two later stopped any discoveries being made.'

Lovelace cut in: 'And this dancing lad? Carter? He went back to Cromer too?'

Posie could only guess this part in the absence of facts.

She shook her head. 'I think Dulcie took my mother's own key to this apartment at the Mermaid before they buried the body, and they hatched a plan. She and Nicky Carter agreed that *he* would return here. Dulcie had grown up here; I bet she knew every inch of the tunnels the Hawkhurst Gang had ever built. She must have smuggled Nicky in from some out-of-town entrance. He began sleeping here, wearing Dulcie's father's old clothes, doing what Dulcie told him to. He needed to be here because they needed to make it look like Rosa had died in a tragic accident nearby, because soon enough she would be missed, and questions would be asked.'

Posie nodded, more certain of her case with each passing second.

'And so Nicky Carter, on Dulcie's instructions, probably late at night on the Sunday or Monday this week, threw a couple of Rosa's things into the quay. He had to place the things in such a way that they would be found, not swept out to sea. And everything went according to plan, which is surprising, as Nicky probably isn't the brightest of lads, and goodness knows why he thought throwing only one lightweight dancing shoe into the river would be convincing, but again, his luck held, and everyone believed the "truth" of what they were seeing when the items were discovered late on Tuesday.'

Posie cast a look of slight reproachfulness over at Inspector Vallance, who blushed slightly.

'Rosa Rossoli was declared dead on Wednesday, which is when the solicitor had to telephone to Dulcie in Cromer with the sad news. And, sure enough, Dulcie answered his call up there, at the Hotel de Paris. Conveniently miles from here. Away from any suspicion.'

Posie almost laughed.

'And all of this dreadful while, Dulcie, and perhaps Nicky, were being eaten up with a simmering jealousy, and rage, and perhaps guilt. I think they were still labouring under some kind of misapprehension that Rosa had changed her Will in favour of me. I'm not sure if it was Nicky, bored here, who discovered the stack of letters my mother had left for me, and who forced the trunk open and read some of them, including one which had details of my friendship with Rufus in it – a newspaper clipping about Dolly's disappearance. Or if it was Dulcie's idea? Either way, it must suddenly have seemed like a good opportunity. They changed tack and decided to include Rufus in their mad plots. *Get Rufus: get me: make some money*. A terrible plan was hatched.'

'So, Miss,' said Fox excitedly, 'you think they only cooked up this plan in the last few days?'

'I do,' Posie replied.

'It was badly handled, although the evil in it was strong enough. I've told you, Nicky Carter doesn't appear to be the smartest fella. Dulcie stayed away and tasked Nicky with sending telegrams to Rufus, in order to get him here, and Nicky did so, but he seems to have lacked any imagination, and sense.'

Posie turned and pointed at the guidebook about Rye on the table.

‘I think Nicky Carter thumbed through that book and came up with one of the first names he came across, and used it as his pseudonym when writing to Rufus. Why else would you call yourself “Thomas Kingsmill”?’

‘But why the two separate telegrams?’ asked Richard Lovelace, askance. ‘One sent to London, and one sent here? And only the second one mentioning *you*? Was that deliberate?’

Posie nodded. ‘Dulcie must have specified it should be like that. I think it was vital to the whole plan that Rufus left first, alone; in a frantic hurry, thinking he might be reunited with Dolly. If *I* had been mentioned in the first telegram, there would always have been the possibility Rufus and I would have spoken together, and I would have involved the police from the start. Or, worse, that we would have travelled down together in Rufus’ car. It was crucial that Rufus went by train, left the car behind.’

Posie explained that the Lagonda was very important.

Because Dulcie had planned to take the car from London and to drive it quite deliberately right off the cliffs. This would add authenticity and a level of confusion when it was revealed that Rufus, Earl of Cardigeon, had gone missing.

It would buy the couple a few days’ grace.

‘Dulcie needed the car for something else, too,’ said Posie, grimly. ‘I think Dulcie drove to the cliff at Hastings yesterday, somehow retrieved my mother’s body from wherever it was she had been buried or hidden six days before, and put it into the Lagonda’s back seat. Dulcie scattered luggage – whatever Rufus had had in the car – all about the place, and then she reversed to the highest point of the steep grass cliff, above Ludlam’s, and jumped out, and let the car zoom away with its dreadful cargo inside.’

‘This is a grisly tale, my love,’ said Richard, askance, and she saw that he hadn’t even opened his cigarette tin, nor clicked his knuckles, not once.

Perhaps because of the gun in his hands, too, which he held firm and steadfastly.

Posie held her head up high.

'It *is* awful, but Dulcie is clever, I'll give her that. I think she came here to the Mermaid last night, after she'd crashed the car, and joined Nicky in this flat. Today I noticed there were *two* teacups in the sink, and the hot-water pipes and the metal of the sink were warm with use. But the cups had disappeared again when Fox went to double-check. It was all evidence of someone, or some people, being in here, despite the fact the place was supposed to be locked up. And using the Mermaid as a *rendezvous* for Rufus to come to was a stroke of inspired genius: a creepy, old, supposedly-haunted place is an easy location to creep around in through a warren of hidden corridors and passageways, and any footsteps and creaking floorboards are automatically ignored.'

She laughed, but it sounded hollow even to her own ears, and there was certainly no joy in it.

'I think Dulcie has been spying on Rufus, and on me, too. Today. Watching through cracks in the walls and the panelling. Hiding in secret passages. I'm pretty certain Dulcie was hidden behind the panelling in the small lounge when I first arrived today, that she even darted out in the open to look at me for a second, and then she was lurking behind the panelling again when I lay down on my bed in the 'Thomas Kingsmill' room. She even had the cheek to blow my scented candle out! But she couldn't trick Patsy, who knew she was there all along.'

Posie pointed at the map in Fox's hands, the only one which Evans had been able to locate today.

'Dulcie planned this all quite well, considering it was thrown together just these last few days. This map was *hers*. I recognised the writing on it earlier as being Dulcie's. She probably made it when she was growing up here, copied it, learnt from it. But last night she doctored the map. I think

Dulcie snuck to reception in the night, along a hidden passageway, and took all the other maps in the desk there and destroyed them. She left *only* this one; from which she had carefully erased most of the tunnels. Especially the tunnel which leads right from the Priest's Hole, up to this very room. So we would never have been able to locate it. And for the exact same reason Dulcie effectively 'kidnapped' Mrs Joab, the Proprietress, after lunch, so Mrs Joab could never be quizzed about the layout of the tunnels; so that Dulcie could spirit Rufus away easily…'

Lovelace's green eyes opened wide. 'Where is this tunnel?' he whispered.

Posie nodded towards the cold, boarded-up fireplace.

'*There.*'

Then she added loudly, clearly: 'Darling, have you got your gun? Fire it straight through the fireplace, won't you? I bet its only thin plaster board covering the mouth of the tunnel. And your men are at the other end, aren't they? Lots of them? Also with guns?'

At Lovelace's inaction and open-mouthed horror, Fox leant across and took the pistol from his boss and fired it once into the ceiling.

Everyone ducked, and Patsy started barking.

'Hey, Fox!'

But Richard's protests were drowned out by Fox letting off another volley of gunshots into the cheap wood, and then suddenly, weirdly, the white, stuccoed fireplace in front of them seemed to concertina back on itself, to reveal itself as a wide, gaping hole in the wall.

And out of it came Rufus, gagged and sweaty and bound, and then the Proprietress, Mrs Joab, also gagged and bound, both of them dusty but otherwise unharmed.

They collapsed onto the floor, terrified but silent.

And then out stepped Posie's sister, clutching at something silver, and last of all her murderous, glamorous wrong'un of a partner.

* * * *

The man looked to be unarmed, and Vallance stepped forward and handcuffed Nicky Carter, who fitted almost exactly his description given by the lady at the Post Office. Except today he was wearing no moustache or sideburns, and his hair was thin, nearly gone, just with a few strands scraped over. So, he'd been helping himself to Benito's props box, too. And today he looked scared. He didn't utter a word, but his hands and arms were shaking uncontrollably.

Fox moved over warily to Dulcie, a set of handcuffs at the ready.

But the girl, gorgeous beneath her fear and frenzy, rammed herself up against the wall, a very sharp silver knife extended in her shaking hands, and Fox backed off.

Richard Lovelace was calm, shaking his head incredulously.

'Where on earth were you going to take the Earl, Miss Rossoli? What were your plans? Wait up here until the fuss had died down, then sell him to the highest bidder?'

Dulcie's small dark eyes were blazing angrily, and she flicked her hair, longer than Posie remembered it, haughtily over her shoulder.

She wore a long-sleeved black woollen dress, plain, without ornament or detail.

'We were going to France, actually,' Dulcie snapped back, sounding brittle.

'We'd arranged a passage out from here on Monday, on a fishing-boat across the marshes. I'd been trying to reach that gang in Paris, the ones who have taken the Earl's drippy little wife. It's been in the newspapers often enough, hasn't it? It wasn't hard to reach them. I placed adverts in the main Paris newspaper, paid a translator to help, asking the gang to contact me here.'

Lovelace laughed easily, and there was real humour in

it now. 'Most of Scotland Yard and the best teams of police in France haven't managed to get hold of that gang, Miss Rossoli, and you thought *you* would succeed?'

'I did succeed!' shouted Dulcie, as Fox tried to edge nearer again.

'I spoke to a jolly nice chap called Caspian, as it happens. He called me here, today, at reception, at three o'clock. It was Mrs Joab's shift anyhow but I'd already taken care of her so the place was empty. You, Chief Commissioner, were busy interviewing that poor wine merchant, and Posie had gone off somewhere, shopping. We had a nice chat. This Caspian fella was interested to hear Posie was here, and well. Very interested. He'd heard she'd been sick. I told him I planned to kill her, was going to kill her as soon as ever I could, but he convinced me not to. Very sweet of him. He said he wouldn't take the Earl here, unless Posie remained alive. Promised me a big fat wodge of cash, too...'

Richard had gone very white under his freckles, and Posie rose from the sofa to grab him, thinking he looked as if he might faint.

'She's lying, sir!' said Inspector Vallance in a flat manner. 'Just goading you, Chief Commissioner. What a piece of work this woman is! And a murderess too! How could she be *here* today taking a call on the telephone if she was larking about in a purple dress on the cliffs at Hastings! *Loitering...*'

'I'm not lying,' snapped Dulcie in a hissing sort of manner, an angry cat, the silver knife flashing.

'I wasn't at Hastings cliffs today. Yesterday, maybe, for a couple of minutes. But what would I be doing there today, in all the snow? Purple? I never wear purple! You must be mad. You can check on the call anyhow, with the Operator, can't you? It came in from Dieppe; a hotel called the Lion D'or. This Caspian fella said they were all there, the Countess of Cardigeon included. But they'd shortly be leaving; returning to Paris.'

Richard nodded at Fox. His mouth was grim.

Suddenly and without another warning, Fox fired several shots in quick succession through to the open door of the bedroom.

PAH, PAH, PAH, PAH.

In all the confusion everyone ducked, and Richard threw himself at Dulcie Rossoli, who had crouched down automatically, and the sudden dead weight of Richard's body falling on top of her caused her to release the knife she had been wielding, just for a second.

But it was enough.

The knife skittered over the floor and Richard grabbed it, passing it to Vallance. He then looped Dulcie's arms behind her back and pulled out his own handcuffs, none too gently, to snap about the girls' slender wrists.

'There! That's better.'

Posie blew out her breath in slow relief. She watched as Richard took out his cigarette tin, all the while supporting Dulcie's flailing, angry dancer's body. He lit a cigarette slowly, taking his time, took a deep drag.

Then he spoke over the top of Dulcie's head, addressing Nicky Carter, too, who was still trembling and couldn't take his eyes off the floor.

'You'll both be taken to Rye Police Station and charged with breach of the peace and attempted kidnapping of both the Earl and Mrs Joab. Until we have Rosa Rossoli's body, and rest assured, we will look and look for it, I cannot charge you with her murder, but it's only a matter of time. I promise you that.'

'I would have let Mrs Joab go,' said Dulcie, huffily. 'After we had got away.'

Posie came closer and stared at Dulcie, meeting her gaze.

'You *were* moving about in corridors and hidden places, spying on me, today, weren't you, Dulcie? Hoping I'd get scared. Once or twice I'm certain I saw a glimmer of that knife. You must have been holding it right up to the cracks of wood.'

The girl grinned maliciously but stayed quiet.

Posie *had* to know. 'Would you really have killed me, Dulcie? With that wretched knife? But what *for*?'

Dulcie's dark eyes flashed with a crazy, mournful sort of fire. #

'Because I tried and tried with you, and you never cared. Never bothered! I sent postcards which you hardly answered, and eventually I gave up! Focused instead on finding another husband for myself. And so far, we've been happy, Nicky and me. Until I heard on Wednesday night last week from our mother on the telephone that *you* were going to get what was rightfully mine. She was going to change her Will to include you. I couldn't believe it! She mentioned it again on Friday, when we met for real. Said she'd already done it...'

'But you misunderstood! The Will has been proved.'

Posie got her carpet bag and grabbed out the copy of Rosa's Will, held it up for Dulcie, who read it slowly.

Dulcie swallowed, frowned very slightly. 'So, you were just getting letters? A pack of letters? So mother spoke the truth, at the end? Before she...before she...'

Posie whispered. 'Before you killed her for nothing. She even went to the special effort of *saying* in the Will that the letters are worth nothing. She must have known you well, Dulcie; known the jealousy you were capable of.'

Dulcie gave an exaggerated sigh.

'All of my childhood memories are of my mother sitting in this freezing cold room, at that table, writing those wretched blue letters. I didn't understand who you were, then, of course. But I knew you must be important: the time and energy she spent on them. They certainly weren't worth nothing to her! I was always jealous of you.'

Posie rolled her eyes in disbelief. 'But you had *her*. You had our mother, Rosa. I had nothing, and I never even got those wretched letters! I don't know why, but she chose never to send them! What a complete waste.'

Dulcie shrugged. She was being manoeuvred along by Fox, nearly at the door now.

She turned abruptly.

'I told Mother about you, of course, when I met you a couple of years back. She didn't act surprised at your success. Said she'd always followed you. I told her to get in touch, but she said she'd ruined your life once: that you had to move on. Oh, and yes: I *was* watching you today, behind the panelling. I know all those old routes. I had the knife held ready. But I swear to God that I never dashed out into the open of the lounge to see you. Nor ran out and blew a candle out. What do you think I am? Reckless? That must have been someone else entirely.'

Posie was speechless, for once. She licked her dry, cracked lips.

She watched Nicky Carter being escorted out of the room, too. Partners who would never dance again.

What a waste. What an abysmal pair.

But her mother had been right.

You had to move on.

* * * *

Epilogue

Posie and Richard stood together by the railing overlooking the quayside. Patsy was back at the hotel, being looked after at reception. Rufus was back in the Giant's Fireside Bar of the Mermaid, drinking, being watched over by Sergeant Fox.

It was completely dark now, and the snow had stopped.

They were eating fish and chips from paper cones and enjoying every bite. At Posie's feet was the trunk bequeathed her by her mother.

They hadn't spoken for several minutes.

At last, it was Lovelace who broke the companionable silence. 'Can you explain that message on the key, Posie? About checking the shoes? I still don't understand *who* wrote it, or *how*. Because without it you would never have insisted on counting those dancing shoes…'

Posie took a breath. 'It wasn't 'check the shoes', darling, was it? It was 'check the pairs'. So anybody could have written that, and about anything.'

In purple ink.

In her mother's hand.

Well, it was possible it had been about something else entirely. Something mundane, domestic.

Apples, pears, tights, laundry, earrings.

Dancing shoes.

'And who or what was the woman in purple?' asked Richard, eating a last mouthful, and scrunching up his paper forcefully.

'It wasn't the mysterious Violette, as I had imagined, and it wasn't the murderous Dulcie. Oh, by the way, I heard tonight that they've managed to hoist the Lagonda up. But it will be morning until they can search it.'

Posie didn't believe in ghosts. Didn't want to. Didn't believe she had the sort of personality which attracted them.

'I don't know who that woman was, or is. Probably the sort of person who makes a nuisance of herself, turning up at strangers' weddings; the sort who is always looking for drama. But she was helpful. She helped me establish what had happened, didn't she? Vallance told me she was there from the moment my mother died, buried shabbily by the bins at a closed café. So I pieced it together from there onwards.'

But there was something about the edges of places - cliffs, mountains, seas - which worried Posie. *Border zones.*

They seemed to attract a sort of magic, a peculiar chemistry of slipping between states, between dimensions.

Once, by the sea near Dover, Posie had been convinced she had seen an ex-boyfriend, certainly dead and drowned, walking along the cliffs. It gave her the shivers, even now, to remember it.

Could that have been her mother on those cliffs? Trying from some other far-off place to bring attention to a heinous crime which had been committed against her; trying to bring attention to where her body was lying?

'I knew about your mother, darling,' said Richard, gently, after a few minutes more silence.

'I knew she was going by the name of 'Rossoli' and that's why mention of the name gave me such a start. I'm probably the most informed man in England, you know.

No point in having secrets from me. I knew she had left your family in Norfolk, started afresh somewhere else. I had no idea it was *here*, though. And I didn't know about Dulcie being your sister. Or that she wrote to you…'

Posie stared at him through the darkness.

He often surprised her. In a good way.

'You never spoke of my mother, Richard. Didn't you want to ask me about her?'

'Why would I? I thought you might bring it up in your own sweet time.'

'She ran away. Did you think I would do the same?'

'Of course not. Everyone is different. No two mothers are alike. And you are wonderful. Our children are so lucky to have you.'

Posie had never wanted to be a mother, had come to it rather by accident, actually. But something very strange had happened.

This year, in July, Posie had discovered she was pregnant again.

And even though Kit was only tiny, she had been flooded with joy and hope and a sense of complete wonder. She had been filled with a longing anticipation for this new child.

And then had come a kind of tragedy, right on top of what had happened to Dolly, when Posie had lost the baby in September.

And she had got sick, and then sicker, and a sort of darkness had come into Posie's life which simply didn't shift.

It had been terrifying.

And it was hopefully now gone. But it had taken time.

Until now, in fact.

'Darling,' said Richard, at her side, looking out at the black, black flatlands.

'It doesn't matter if we don't have another baby. We have so much. And even if we didn't have Phyllis, or Katie, or Kit, I'd be the luckiest man in the world to have *you*.'

Posie smiled and looped her arm through his, squeezed him tightly.

Along the quayside a man was throwing things onto a huge bonfire.

A few people were grouped about, watching. Its orange flames ripped up into the sky and spotted the air with twinkles.

At Posie's feet was the trunk and she kicked at it gently. She'd had in mind to throw it in the water, and Richard, eyebrows raised quizzically, had carried it out for her unquestioningly.

They moved, rather hypnotically, towards the fire, and watched it for a few minutes.

They would be returning home in the morning.

'You can't have a fire as big as this in London, can you?' Posie asked.

She was pulling open the trunk now, and stepping closer to the fire, and reaching into the trunk and pulling out handful after handful of her mother's unsent letters, watching the dry old paper with all that lost love, spilled ink, spilled tears and wasted time splinter and curl in seconds; sending up scurrying sparks of orange into the blackness.

You will always be my mother, Posie thought to herself.

She suddenly remembered Evans talking about the missing mermaid ship-prow, and how the name lingered on. Perhaps the same could be said of her unusual mother?

'*When the legend of something is strong enough, it doesn't matter if the original is long gone. It lives on anyhow.*'

But her mother had been right. Posie did need to move on.

There is so much to do.

Christmas.

And presents.

She promised herself suddenly that tomorrow morning, before leaving, she would walk to the gallery on the High

Street and buy the painting she had seen of Rye. She would treat herself to it, hang it in her office, and use it as a way to remember her mother. In a good way.

And next, she would have to address Dolly's disappearance. Go to Paris.

I have to find Dolly.

But Richard was talking again. Posie couldn't hear him properly above the roar of the fire.

'What, darling?'

'I said I hope you're not going to leave me, Posie.'

She looked at him, askance. She saw his mouth, mock serious, trying not to laugh.

'Why would I leave you?'

'I think you will want to go to Paris fairly soon. To look for Dolly. Perhaps you'll go off with an eighteen-year-old French lad, at the same time? A Count, eh? And a handsome one at that. I'd better watch my step.'

Posie's face burned a shameful red in the heat of the fire. 'Listen, I never wrote him a thing, Richard. And how the blazes do you know about…'

Richard laughed. 'I told you, I'm the best-informed man in England. I haven't ever read anything of yours, darling. I just know these adoring missives exist.'

'I see. Well, not for much longer.'

And then Posie was digging in her carpet bag and taking out the letters she had been meaning to get rid of for ages. Anatole's silly love letters.

She threw them on the fire and they made a satisfying hiss.

For a second Posie thought she saw a woman with a sparkling, purple, sequined hat like a turban, and dark eyes trying to catch her eye, standing on the other side of the fire, with her back to the water of the canal, a slender umbrella in her hand, like a walking stick.

And then, looking further along the quayside, in the

dim glow of a street-lamp, Posie thought she saw a couple dancing, close together, two dark heads in unison, a purple dress flowing in the cold night wind, a flash of cheap paste jewels, a flick of a feather boa. The man in a brown suit.

But Posie turned away quickly, her heart beating fast.

Next I'll say I've seen mermaids swimming in the bay.

And as they turned to walk back up Mermaid Street, with Richard carrying the empty trunk, it seemed that life and love had come together very nicely right now, and that anything out there on a border zone – anything remotely magical – could stay exactly where it was.

Until the next time, anyhow.

'Oh, Posie darling?'

'Mnnn?'

'Fox told me he heard Rufus on the telephone, in reception, before we left the Mermaid for our fish and chips earlier. Seems the Earl is so distraught about losing his Lagonda that he's already ordered himself a new one.'

'That's jolly nice.'

'Isn't it? And Fox said the order was for *two*. The second Lagonda is to be delivered to you. So, it seems you'll be driving for real soon again, after all, eh? Not just in those pesky dreams of yours. Super, eh? I've always fancied being driven in a fast car by a beautiful woman...'

And as they went in under the sign of the caged Mermaid, swinging slightly in the wind which was getting up, Posie couldn't take the grin off her face.

She hadn't felt so good in ages.

But perhaps, after all, she *was* slightly like her mother, she realised now.

She would never, ever run away from her children.

But she did have this perverse desire to get away sometimes. To leave everything, however wonderful, behind.

I want to drive again, she whispered to herself.

She smiled.
I want to be free.

****

Acknowledgements

Thank you to my parents who took me to Rye in the first place and helped me discover this town which seems 'wholly of the past'.

I thank also my husband and daughters for the trip we paid to the Mermaid in Rye back in the strange but wonderful summer of 2021.

Thank you to the genealogical mystery writer Nathan Dylan Goodwin for his time and generosity in sharing some newspaper resources relating to Rye with me.

For his books, see: https://www.nathandylangoodwin.com

I would also like to mention the artist Richard Adams, whose fantastic and much sought-after paintings of the English and their quirkily-observed habits within the countryside are all mainly of Rye (and many feature mermaids) and these have always been an inspiration and point of reference for me. See the photographs section, and find him here: https://www.ryebank.gallery/richard-adams

Thank you also to Judith Blincow, the owner of the Mermaid Inn in Rye for meeting me, answering questions, and allowing me to use the wonderful location of her hotel for this story.

See: https://www.mermaidinn.com/

Pictures

1.) The Mermaid Inn, Mermaid Street, Rye

2.) Going uphill to the Mermaid Inn, Rye

3.) Painting by Richard Adams entitled
'Ticket to Rye', 2021

Historical Note

All of the characters in this novella are fictional, unless specifically mentioned below.

Weather, timings, general political events, and places (and descriptions of places) are historically accurate to the best of my knowledge, save for the exceptions listed below.

As in the other Posie Parker books, I refer to the First World War of 1914–1918 as the 'Great War' throughout, which is simpler for the modern reader, although it would not have been referred to in this way in 1925.

As ever, Posie's work address in London (Grape Street, Bloomsbury, WC1) and her home address around the corner (Museum Chambers, WC1) are both very real, although you might have to do a bit of imagining to find her there.

The Mermaid Inn, as described in this story is, of course, very real and has carved its own piece of rich history for over five hundred years in the East Sussex port town of Rye. It has cellars dating from 1156 and the inn as it stands today was rebuilt in 1420, its original incarnation (together with the whole town of Rye) having been burnt to the ground by French raiders in 1377.

Most famous for being the meeting-point of the infamous and violent Hawkhurst Gang of smugglers (whose activity at the inn is dated around 1735–1749), it is reported to be haunted by a collection of ghosts associated with this gang.

It is an inn which has attracted royalty and famous personages (including Shakespeare himself) through the ages, it is a uniquely riveting place, heavy with the feel of its own history, and yet it is also a wonderfully warm and welcoming place for the modern-day visitor. The superb restaurant and luxury rooms are certainly unforgettable. See: https://www.mermaidinn.com/

1. (Chapter Three) The book I describe Lovelace handing to Posie, *Patterson's Guide to Smuggling and Tax Evasion: History and Legal Precedents*, is completely fictional. But *Highways & Byways in Sussex* by E. V. Lucas (published 1919), which Posie reads on the train to Rye, was very real. Second-hand copies can still be obtained, although they are, by now, rare, and collector's editions.

2. (Chapter Three) The train journey from London to Rye on a Southern Railway train which Posie and Richard undertake would actually have included a change at Ashford in Kent, or at Hastings in Sussex, which for the sake of brevity and the story arc I do not mention here. The train journey remains the same today.

3. (Chapter Three and throughout) The story of Rosa Parker, Posie's mother, and the full mystery behind why she left the Parker family in 1903 is explored more fully in the stand-alone novella by L. B. Hathaway, *A Christmas Case: A Posie Parker Novella*.

4. (Chapter Four) For the High Street in Rye and in particular The George Hotel, I have used E.V. Lucas' description in *Highways & Byways in Sussex*. For the

same hotel today see: https://thegeorgeinrye.com

5. (Chapter Four) The painting which Posie looks at in the window of a gallery in the High Street is based on a contemporary one, by local artist Richard Adams, entitled *Ticket to Rye* (see the previous section). I have described the picture as is, but I have added the dancing couple on the quay as a plot device all of my own.

6. (Chapter Five and throughout) The Proprietress, Mrs Joab, and the receptionist, Evans, at the Mermaid are both fictional. Please note I have gone for an atmospheric rather than a strictly historical approach when describing the appearance and layout of the Mermaid. I have described it as if the visitor was entering the hotel today, rather than in the year 1925, when this novel is set.

7. (Chapter Five) The story I give for the naming of the Mermaid is entirely fictional and my own conjecture.

8. (Throughout) The storyline regarding Rosa Rossoli, the summer tea-dances at the Mermaid and her living arrangements there, and the story of the crashed Lagonda at Hastings cliffs are all completely fictional, as is the story of Rosa's disappearance in the *Sussex Express* of 2 December 1925. The other stories and adverts I mention as being in that same newspaper are, however, accurate as to that day's edition.

9. (Chapter Six and Seven) The snowy, sleety funeral of the much-loved Queen Alexandra did take place in London on 27 November 1925. It was echoed all around the country, such as in St Mary's Church,

Rye, so people could feel they were participating in marking the much-loved Queen's death.

10. (Chapter Six) Melville & Sons on Rye High Street (solicitors) is fictional. The Probate Registry which Mr Putebank refers to as being in Rye would have been accurate at this date, but was abolished and moved to Battle in 1931.

11. (Chapter Nine) There is indeed a heat-sealed Priest's Hole in the fireplace of the Giant's Bar, however, the staff apartments upstairs (including room 32) and the connecting tunnels to this particular Priest's Hole are a fancy of my own. As indeed are the maps illustrating these.

****

Thank you for joining Posie Parker and her friends.

Enjoyed *Murder and the Mermaid* (A Posie Parker Mystery #13)? Here's what you can do next.

If you loved this book and have a tiny moment to spare, I would really appreciate a review or rating on the page where you bought the book. Your help in spreading the word about the series is invaluable and really appreciated, and reviews make a big difference to helping new readers find the series.

Posie's other cases are available in e-book and paperback formats from Amazon, as well as in selected bookstores and at Audible and other main audiobook retailers. You can find all of the other books, available for purchase, listed here in chronological order:

http://www.amazon.com/L.B.-Hathaway/e/B00LDXGKE8

and

http://www.amazon.co.uk/L.B.-Hathaway/e/B00LDXGKE8

You can sign up to be notified of new releases, pre-release specials, free short stories, and the chance to win Amazon gift-vouchers here:

http://www.lbhathaway.com/newsletter/

About the Author

Cambridge-educated, British-born L.B. Hathaway writes historical fiction. She worked as a lawyer at Lincoln's Inn in London for almost a decade before becoming a full-time writer. She is a lifelong fan of detective novels set in the Golden Age of Crime, and is an ardent Agatha Christie devotee.

Her other interests, in no particular order, are: very fast downhill skiing, theatre-going, drinking strong tea, Tudor history, exploring castles and generally trying to cram as much into life as possible. She lives in Switzerland with her husband and young family.

The Posie Parker series of cosy crime novels span the 1920s. They each combine a core central mystery, an exploration of the reckless glamour of the age and a feisty protagonist who you would love to have as your best friend.

To find out more and for news of new releases and giveaways, go to:

http://www.lbhathaway.com

Connect with L.B. Hathaway online:

(e) author@lbhathaway.com

(t) @LbHathaway

(f) https://www.facebook.com/pages/L-B-Hathaway-books/1423516601228019

(Goodreads) http://www.goodreads.com/author/show/8339051.L_B_Hathaway

Printed in Great Britain
by Amazon

18027653R00082